Later that week I heard a knock on my door. It was the landlord. "You're three days late with your rent."

"I put it in your mail slot on the first of the month."

He rolled his eyes at me. "You think I'd be here if you'd paid?"

He coughed as he sometimes did since he was a smoker and the stench from his breath was revolting.

"I paid my rent. I saw you with my check in your hand the very day I dropped it off. Maybe you misplaced it?"

It looked like maybe he was starting to become angry because one of his eyebrows began to twitch. "Don't know what you're talking about," he said then stumbled a bit and braced himself against the doorframe. Then he added, after righting himself, "You think I like coming around here like this?" I couldn't say whether he liked it or not, but his tone suggested he didn't. He didn't seem to know what to say next, but eventually said, "How 'bout you just give me a new check?"

I decided that it wasn't worth the bother and went to get my checkbook. Unfortunately, I'd just used my last few checks on some bills. When I told him this, he didn't seem to believe me, and it perhaps even bolstered his belief that I was lying to him.

He left without saying anything further, but the way he looked at me as he did, and the way he looked at Molly, gave me the greatest urge to see him red and open.

A vacuum salesman by day, the introvert lives a quiet life alone with his dog until a work relationship and a dark secret from his past team up to create an uncomfortable imbalance in his otherwise ordered life, one that soon finds him squarely at the center of a murder investigation. With his thoughts continually urging him to make people "red and open" and to "achieve it" with his girlfriend Donna, what follows is a sometimes brutal, oftentimes hilarious, and absurdist account of the life of one very anti-social and unexpected anti-hero.

KUDOS for *The Introvert*

The story is cute, poignant, and thought-provoking. I loved it. ~ *Taylor Jones, Reviewer*

I rarely like stories which have an anti-hero, but I couldn't help rooting for this one. I read it twice, just for the sheer enjoyment of it. ~ *Regan Murphy, Reviewer*

THE
INTROVERT

MICHAEL PAUL MICHAUD

A Black Opal Books Publication

GENRE: MYSTERY-DETECTIVE/SUSPENSE

THE INTROVERT
Copyright © 2016 by Michael Paul Michaud
Cover Design by Michael Paul Michaud
All cover art copyright © 2016
All Rights Reserved
Print ISBN: 978-1-626945-47-0

First Publication: NOVEMBER 2016

Published by Black Opal Books **http://www.blackopalbooks.com**

For the weirdos

THE
INTROVERT

The Company Culture Handbook

Always Stay Positive
Every Day is a Good Day to Buy
Set Your Clock to Lombardi Time
Be a Humble Student
Assault Them with Honesty
Always Diffuse Discomfort
Control the Conversation
Nobody Likes a Challenger
Dress the Part
The Company is Your Friend

CHAPTER 1

Sir, have you got a second form of identification?"

She was looking at me from her seated position behind the counter. She wasn't much of a clerk. From what I could see, she was shabbily dressed, and there was a half-eaten container of Chinese noodles on the counter with a plastic fork sticking out from the cardboard box, and since it was morning, I figured that it must have been leftovers.

"You have my driver's license," I said.

The woman behind the counter smiled, and I wasn't sure why because to me she didn't seem very happy.

"Yes sir, but I do need to see a second form of identification."

"I'm just renewing my license," I said, and I thought that might settle things.

"Sir, I'm afraid we require a second form of identification before we can proceed. If you'd like to come back another time, perhaps?" She was still smiling, but now the smile was waning.

I turned to look at the line behind me that snaked back to the door where I'd first been standing when I'd come in almost forty minutes ago. Then I turned back to face the clerk, but for some reason my eyes caught again on the cardboard container of Chinese noodles and the white plastic instrument peeking up over the edge, and it made me nauseous just to see it.

"Sir?"

When I looked back up, I saw that her smile was all the way gone.

"My license expires tomorrow," I said, looking again at the noodles.

I needed my license to drive my car legally. It wasn't much of a car, but I still needed a valid driver's license to drive it.

"I understand that, sir, but I'm afraid we do require a second form of identification."

I brought my eyes to her face and stared blankly at the fat sphere in front of me and noticed that the lipstick on her lips was red and the mole on her neck was brown, and though both were hideous they at least made me briefly forget about the Chinese noodles. "I have credit cards," I said.

I could hear people grumbling behind me when I said this.

"I'm afraid that isn't sufficient, sir."

It was the third time that she'd said she was afraid, only she didn't seem afraid. I'd seen people afraid before and their eyes usually went wide and open and white and their mouths gaped sloppy or crooked.

"I have to be at work in ten minutes."

I wasn't exactly sure why I said it since it didn't seem entirely connected to what we were talking about. But then if she'd have just allowed me to renew my driver's license then I probably wouldn't have been worrying about being late for work, so then I thought that maybe it was a little bit connected after all, if not all the way connected.

"Sir, perhaps if you came back another time?"

I could tell that she was trying to get rid of me.

"Why would someone who isn't me ever want to renew my license?"

"Sir, I can't comment on that. But we do have our regulations…"

I could hear the sighs and the grumbles growing heavier behind me so I fished in my wallet for some other form of government identification though I knew it was hopeless even before I tried.

When I looked back up I could see the clerk staring at me and the smile was back on her face now and even enhanced in a way that it hadn't been before, as if perhaps with more fake friendliness I might go away faster and then she could take another bite from her container with the plastic fork or move onto the next customer or both.

A man stepped up to the wicket to my right. He'd been one of the people staring at me when I'd last turned around so I was relieved that he was now being served, but then I figured there were many others still staring just as intently so I didn't feel relieved for very long.

The clerk continued to smile at me, and I thought again how she wasn't much of a clerk. It wasn't very professional to have opened food at the counter. It wasn't very nice to smile at people when you didn't really mean it. Finally, she apologized once more and slid my expiring license back toward me on the counter.

That was when I noticed the letter opener.

It was resting in front of her, long and steel and quite clearly sharp at one end, all shiny and polished and silver. It was easily within reach, and before I knew it I was again thinking of how she was making me late for work and how the boss wouldn't like that. Then I imagined picking up the letter opener and stabbing down viciously into her plump pasty white neck and how I wanted more than anything in that moment to see her red and open.

Red and open.

And I thought that I'd have to thrust the opener with real force to pierce the thick layer of fat around her neck and I imagined how the blood would be gushing out red and wet and slide down over her hideous brown mole and how then she really would be afraid with her eyes opened wide in fear and her mouth twisted apart and how people would be running in fear behind me and there would be screams and gasps and commotion all around and how the clerk would be wishing she'd have just let me renew my driver's license before she succumbed to the attack only by then it would be too late.

"Sir?"

It felt good to think it, but instead I just picked up my driver's license from the counter and turned away because I knew that she didn't deserve it.

She wasn't much of a clerk, but she certainly didn't deserve it.

CHAPTER 2

I was late for my job.

It wasn't much of a job. I sold vacuum cleaners to people who mostly already had vacuum cleaners. Our brand was decent enough and had a good reputation in the community. I even had one myself and was able to purchase it at cost because I worked for the company. I'm not sure if I would have purchased it otherwise, but I figured I still probably would have.

Part of our sales pitch to customers was that vacuum technology was always changing and resulting in better health for your family by trapping a higher percentage of dust-motes and dangerous bacteria, which basically said to them that they should buy new vacuums every few years or else it demonstrated that they didn't really care if their family got sick or died from too many dust-motes or dangerous bacteria. I found this to be somewhat disingenuous since in the eight years I'd worked there I hadn't noticed any technological advancements between our older models and our newer models, but I didn't complain about it because the bosses seemed to believe it was true, and maybe there was something more to it than I understood since I didn't actually make them.

My boss for the last three years was a man named Mr. Peters. Before him there were others and most of them treated us like children and Mr. Peters wasn't much different, though he was usually decent enough to me because I usually sold enough vacuums to keep him out of trouble with his own bosses. I think maybe I was successful in sales because I didn't talk very much. Most of my co-workers talked a lot, and if I could barely stand listening to them for free, I could only imagine how the customers would feel about paying for it.

I was fifteen minutes late for my shift when I finally settled into my third-floor cubicle. I worked in the sales office and most of our business was done by phone, although sometimes I went out to people's houses, too. We also had retail outlets where people would actually come in and look at the vacuums, but I'd never wanted to work in those places because I found it easier to talk to people through a telephone receiver than I did talking to people through their actual faces.

I heard Donna say, "Peters came around already," from the cubicle to my right.

I didn't respond. Instead, I logged onto my computer and pulled up my contacts. Half of this job was following up with people who'd previously purchased a vacuum or had expressed at least some mild interest during cold calls. I'd only been working for five minutes before Mr. Peters came up beside me and waited there until I finished my call.

"Good afternoon," he said after I'd hung up the receiver.

This was his way of telling me that I was late since it was fifteen minutes past nine and I was supposed to be ready for work at nine o'clock if not sooner. This comment seemed disrespectful to me, but then maybe he felt the same way about me arriving late, so I figured it was nothing to get too fussed about.

"I'm sorry. I had to go to the DMV."

He just looked at me until I was forced to say more.

"There was a long line, and then the lady at the counter gave me some trouble."

"Trouble at the DMV, eh? You losing your license or something?"

"No," I said.

"You know what the third rule says, don't you?"

He was referring to the third rule of *The Company Culture Handbook*.

"'Set your clock to Lombardi time,'" I said.

"Set Your Clock to Lombardi Time" was corporate jargon for arriving to work fifteen minutes early. That way even if you ran a bit late like I had this morning then you wouldn't really be late at all. It had something to do with Vince Lombardi, who used to coach the Green Bay Packers, but none of that meant anything to me because I didn't watch sports and because I normally did arrive on time or early except maybe when I had to go to the DMV and argue with the woman with the red lipstick and the brown mole or the one time I got a flat tire because of a nail in the road.

Mr. Peters tapped the top of my cubicle three or four times just to show me who was boss but then finally walked away. He hadn't gone very far before I heard Donna's voice.

"Well, that wasn't so bad."

I looked up to see her peeking over from her cubicle. Her arms were up on the divider and her elbows were turned out at each side. She was younger than me. Her hair was blonde but not as blonde as it actually appeared to be. At least it wasn't blonde like that two years ago when she first joined the company.

"Not so bad," I said. I already had the phone back in my hand and was preparing to make my next call.

"So what's wrong with your license?"

Donna always wanted to chat. She'd asked me out on

dates several times before but I hadn't gone yet and I'm not sure why except for the fact that I normally liked to be alone.

"It expires tomorrow," I said.

"Better get it renewed then," she said, which was rather obvious. Now she was tapping the top of the divider between us much in the way that Mr. Peters had done before he left, and even though she wasn't doing it to make me uncomfortable like when Mr. Peters did, I still found it distracting.

"I tried this morning," I said. "The woman told me I needed a second form of identification."

"Yeah, well, there's always something with those places," she said. "Thankfully it only comes around every five years or so. Why'd you leave it so long, anyway?"

I didn't have a very good answer for this so I just shrugged, then I started typing a phone number into the keypad, but Donna kept talking.

"So why didn't you come out on Friday?"

Friday was payday for our company and most of the employees got together after work at a nearby pub called Wellington's. I'd come out once in a while but mostly tried to avoid it. Every time I went out, Donna would come close to my side and touch me on my arm or my leg, and even though she was pretty, it still made me uncomfortable. I knew Jeff wanted to have sex with her, not just because of how he'd stare at her every time she walked past him, but because he'd also told me so on several occasions, usually when he'd been drinking. There were others who looked at her the same way but she didn't seem very interested in them. The way it seemed with girls was that the more attention you paid to them the less they wanted you, and the less attention you paid to them the more they seemed to. Women didn't make much sense that way. Or in a lot of other ways.

"I was tired," was all I said. I started to re-dial the number but she went on anyway.

"It was a good time. Gary bought us each a couple rounds. His deal went through."

Gary had some sort of relationship with a local cleaning plant. For some reason they needed to buy two dozen vacuums every year and Gary had been lucky enough to take the call when they'd phoned in about five years ago. It was a good commission. It also struck me that the deals always went through in a month when there was a contest, like this month, where the top salesman received a bonus of five hundred dollars. I didn't think it was very fair of him to do that, but then I figured I might do the same thing in his place, so I wasn't too fussed about it.

"That's good for him," I said. Then, sensing that Donna wasn't prepared to stop talking anytime soon, I set the receiver back down onto the cradle.

"Anyway, sorry about the contest."

I looked over at the dry-erase white board that hung to the side. Gary was now ahead by eleven vacuums with just eight days remaining.

"The month isn't over," I said.

"No, that's true. So why didn't you come out on Friday?"

I'd thought we'd moved past it, but apparently we hadn't. The truth was I didn't like spending any more time with my co-workers than I absolutely had to. Most of them were decent enough, but I just preferred to be alone. I'd also been wary of alcohol ever since the incident two years ago, and they always pressured me to drink.

"I was tired," I said.

"Aww, but you had all weekend to rest."

"I suppose."

"Will you come out this week?"

"Maybe," I said. By then I had the receiver back in my hand, but it didn't seem to dissuade her.

"Promise me you'll come out this week."

"Okay, I promise," I said, immediately regretting it, though at least she then retreated back to her own cubicle and left me free to dial.

It rang three times before a husky-voiced woman picked up on the other side.

"Good morning, ma'am. I wonder if you'd have a moment to discuss the latest in vacuum technology?"

CHAPTER 3

I arrived home to my apartment just in time to let the dog out before she had an accident.

The dog's name was Molly and I'd found her the same night of the incident. I'm not sure if her name was actually Molly back then, but that's what I started to call her once I figured out that she was a girl, and she didn't seem to mind it. The veterinarian had said that she was some sort of Cocker Spaniel mix, only she didn't tell me what the other part of the mix was, so to me she was just Molly the Cocker Spaniel.

After Molly did her business, we went right back inside because it was cold and wet out. There was one time when Molly didn't last before I got home, and I found the results on the kitchen floor, and it made me so angry that

I thought about making Molly red and open, but then I figured it wasn't her fault and swore to myself to never think of her that way again.

I still regretted promising Donna that I'd go with them to Wellington's on Friday, but then I felt promises should only be broken in the most extreme cases, so I figured I'd have to go and that she'd likely touch my arm and my leg and try to get me to drink alcohol while Jeff and Gary and all the other men stared at her whenever she walked past.

I changed out of my suit and made myself some dinner. I'd only sold two vacuums that day, one through a cold call and one to a friend of a customer who'd purchased one three weeks ago. Gary had also sold two that day, so I remained eleven sales behind with just seven sales days left.

I sat on the couch after dinner and relaxed in my apartment. It wasn't much of an apartment, but I still liked being there more than anywhere else. I didn't have much in the way of property, but I did have a picture of me with my parents when I was young and when we had a Golden Retriever named Shelby, and even Shelby was in the picture. It was the only picture I had of my parents, but that was all right because it was my favorite. I kept it on my dresser in the bedroom, and even if it wasn't much of a dresser, it held up the picture well enough and I could see both my parents smiling in the picture, and I think Shelby was smiling in her own way too because of how her mouth was open and the way her tongue lagged out. Either that or she was just hot, though I suppose it could have been both.

I felt calm and comfortable in my apartment and rarely had the thoughts that I often had in the outside world. The closest I'd come to feeling those thoughts at home was when Molly had her accident on the kitchen floor and the time when my rent was two days late and the landlord knocked on my door looking for it. I answered the door wearing pajamas and no socks and Molly was excited and gyrating at my feet as dogs sometimes do.

"This isn't a flop house," is what he'd said to me.

I'd never been late with the rent before and kept quiet and to myself most of the time, save for when Molly would get excited and bark as she was then doing.

"It's been a tough month at work," I said.

I remember how he'd looked down at Molly and how his face bent nastier than it already was.

"You know we get complaints about that dog sometimes."

"Is this about the rent or about my dog?" I asked.

He wasn't much of a landlord. He was probably in his mid-fifties and I could smell the alcohol on his breath, and it looked like he hadn't shaved in days. He had his own dog that he'd sometimes berate in public or pull vi-

ciously on the leash to make it heel even when it was already heeling. Whenever I saw this I wanted to say something, but then I usually just said something in my mind
and then he would pass by us and then it would be too
late.

"The rent," he'd responded.

"I get paid on Friday," I said.

"Then it will be four days late," he said.

I thought that it was better to be late than never, then
I said it, but the landlord didn't seem to share my opti-
mism.

"There are plenty of people who'd love to get into
this building," he said.

It was probably true. It was a decent price for what
you got, especially in the city.

"And it would be nice to have less weirdos in here,"
he added.

Just like his tone, I felt his last comment to be entirely unnecessary. It wasn't the first time I'd thought of him
as red and open, but it had been the first time I felt it so
intensely. I could see that there was nobody else in the
hallway and I remember how I'd looked down at my bare
feet and how I'd wished I'd been wearing some type of
steel-toed boot because then I could have pulled him inside my apartment and driven him to the ground and
kicked him in the head over and over and over again until
all of his teeth had been knocked out and washed to the

floor in a pool of his own blood and saliva, and how I'd smash his nose into his skull and close off his eyes and how by the time I was done with him his head would be a red and purplish mess and how Molly would likely be barking throughout and annoying the neighbors and then probably run through the mess and track red paw prints around my apartment and how I'd somehow have to clean it up and get rid of the body.

Only I wasn't wearing steel-toed boots, I was barefoot, and before I could decide what to do next he'd already stumbled away and stepped into the stairwell.

e/ɔe/ɔ

I went early to the DMV the next morning and was third in line by the time the doors opened. I was waited on by a young male clerk who I found much more agreeable than the mole-necked clerk from the previous day and I provided him a second form of identification and managed to get my driver's license renewed for an additional five years. Then I thought to myself that it might be nice to go out and celebrate that weekend, so I no longer regretted my promise to Donna.

CHAPTER 4

On Friday I found myself sitting at Wellington's around a large table with ten of my fellow colleagues. It wasn't much of a bar because it was dark and loud and the glasses weren't always clean, but at least they had free peanuts.

I'd pulled to within seven vacuums of Gary by then, but Monday was the final day of the month so it would be hopeless unless I worked through the weekend, which I usually didn't do.

Gary bought everyone a round of beer and though I had mostly avoided alcohol since the incident two years ago, I took one because it was free and because I still felt good about renewing my license on Tuesday and even about coming in second place because it always made

Mr. Peters happy and made for easier days at work.

I'd only finished half of my beer before Donna pulled up a chair beside me, and it wasn't long after that that she was laughing at everything I said, which wasn't very much.

"I like men who keep their word," she said.

"So do I," I said.

"But not in the same way, I bet."

I wasn't exactly sure what she meant by that so I didn't say anything else and instead took another sip of my free beer.

"So were you looking forward to tonight?" She touched my arm for the first time that night.

I said that I was, because it was true, and she seemed to like this very much.

I'd actually showed up late because I had to go home first and take Molly out or risk coming home to another accident on the kitchen floor, and though I knew that it wouldn't be her fault if she had another accident, I knew that it would still make me angry and that it wouldn't be fair to Molly and that it really wouldn't be good for anyone. So instead I went home and took her out and then took a cab to Wellington's just in case I consumed too much alcohol and wasn't fit to drive home.

"I'm glad you came," she said, only this was just as obvious as when she'd told me I better get my license renewed, not only because of how she'd already curled up to me but given the fact that my coming had been her idea in the first place.

"So how's your weekend looking?" she asked.

"I'm not sure. Maybe I'll make some calls."

"Boring," she said.

"There's not much to do on the weekend," I said. "Mostly I take the dog for walks and watch television."

"Sounds lonely."

"No, I have the dog with me," I said, thinking maybe she hadn't heard me the first time.

She just laughed and touched my leg. Donna had recently been seeing some boy in the suburbs, but apparently it hadn't gone well. Whenever one of her relationships ended, she would always tell me how the men were jerks or used her for sex or both and then would ask why she couldn't find a sweet guy like me, and I would tell her I didn't know and then she would laugh and call me modest and I would laugh along with her even though I wasn't actually trying to be modest or funny but truthfully just didn't know the answer.

Tonight she wasn't drinking beer. She was drinking something that was red and purple like the way I'd imagined the landlord's face under steel-toed boots when he'd come up to complain about my rent being two days late. She seemed to enjoy it, and we both finished our drinks rather quickly.

"Buy me another?" she said.

"Okay."

I let her order another drink when the waitress came by then ordered another for myself because Donna said she hated to drink alone. I told her that there were plenty of other people drinking at our table, including the men who would leer at her each time she got up from the table, only I left that last part off. But she said that it wasn't the same, so I ordered another beer and we drank our drinks together once they came. By then I was starting to feel good and thinking that maybe I wouldn't work that weekend after all.

By the end of the third beer, I started to think of the incident from two years ago because the last time I'd felt this intoxicated was when it happened. Donna was touching my arms and legs evenly up to that point, usually when she was laughing at whatever I'd just said, and no matter if it was meant to be funny or not. I could tell that Jeff and Gary weren't happy with the attention that she was paying me because of the looks on their faces each time that she touched me. I didn't much care if Gary felt bad because he was married, and he would be receiving the bonus. I felt a bit different for Jeff since he seemed to genuinely like her, but then I figured that she might like him better if he stopped leering at her, and then I didn't feel so bad for him anymore.

I tried to stop drinking after my third beer, but somehow Donna convinced me to have another. I think maybe

I complied for lack of willpower. Only by then I was also looking at Donna differently. I was noticing her breasts peeking out from beneath her blouse in a way that I never had before, and I was finding myself joining Jeff and Gary in leering at her from behind whenever she stood up and walked to the bathroom. I then started to wonder if Molly might need to be let out again but then Donna returned from one of her bathroom breaks and my focus returned to her blouse and what was beneath it, and I felt that peculiar feeling from down below and hoped that this night wouldn't end up the same way as the last time I'd consumed that much alcohol.

I drank two more beers before I told Donna that I wanted to leave. She suggested we walk or cab home together and I didn't object. We'd hardly walked one block before she took my hand and started to kiss me. Her tongue was cool and tasted like berries. From there we shared a cab back to my place and I was happy to find there was no mess on the kitchen floor and even happier to see what was under Donna's blouse.

It had been a long time since I did the things that I did that night. I don't know why I didn't pursue it more often, because it felt really good, even if it didn't last very long. Donna didn't seem to mind how long it lasted. She curled up around me and fell asleep moments after I'd achieved it. After a few minutes I decided that I wanted to do it again but felt it wouldn't be right to wake her,

so I decided to wait until the morning when she helped
me to achieve it a second time.

CHAPTER 5

Monday seemed no different to me, except that Donna wasn't behaving as she usually did. She asked me why I hadn't called her and I explained that I didn't have her number and that I had no reason to call her. She seemed upset by one or both of these statements, but by lunchtime seemed to have forgotten all about it because she was being friendly as usual.

She gave me her phone number and asked me to call her, but when I asked her what we'd talk about she didn't seem to know, and so we didn't discuss it any further.

I went home at the stroke of five because I was still tired from the weekend. I dropped the month's rent through the slot in the landlord's door on the first floor and then took Molly out for a walk. On our way back in, I saw the landlord chatting with another tenant in the front lobby and I could see him holding my check in his hand.

Molly and I went on upstairs and I didn't give it another moment's thought. Later that week I heard a knock on my door. It was the landlord.

"You're three days late with your rent."

Molly had come up by my side, only this time she was better behaved. Since our last encounter with the landlord several months ago, she'd become wearier of his presence.

"I put it in your mail slot on the first of the month."

He rolled his eyes at me. "You think I'd be here if you'd paid?"

He coughed as he sometimes did since he was a smoker and the stench from his breath was revolting.

"I paid my rent. I saw you with my check in your hand the very day I dropped it off. Maybe you misplaced it?"

It looked like maybe he was starting to become angry because one of his eyebrows began to twitch. "Don't know what you're talking about," he said, then stumbled a bit and braced himself against the doorframe. Then he added, after righting himself, "You think I like coming around here like this?"

I couldn't say whether he liked it or not, but his tone suggested he didn't.

"There's something wrong with my sink," is all I said in reply.

I wasn't trying to change the subject, but I really wasn't worried about my rent since I knew that I'd paid it and the broken sink had just popped into my head. The pipes were old and rusted and had started to leak beneath the sink and I had to use buckets.

"What are you talkin' about, your sink? What's wrong with it?"

"It leaks," I said.

"Well, what'd you do to it?"

"I didn't do anything. I just turned it on and off and it started to leak."

Then he got a searching look on his face. "Hey, didn't I just fix your sink last year?"

"You did. But it was not fixed for long."

"You being smart with me?"

"No," I said.

He didn't seem to know what to say next, but eventually said, "How 'bout you just give me a new check?"

I decided that it wasn't worth the bother and went to get my checkbook. Unfortunately I'd just used my last few checks on some bills. When I told him this, he didn't seem to believe me, and it perhaps even bolstered his belief that I was lying to him.

"What about the sink?" I asked.

He left without saying anything further, but the way

he looked at me as he did, and the way he looked at Molly, gave me the greatest urge to see him red and open.

CHAPTER 6

I went to work the next day and sold five vacuum cleaners. Three were to relatives of former clients, one was from a cold call, and one was from someone who called our company looking to buy one. The last one is what we call a "lay down" because the customer just lies down in front of you with their wallet out. These were the easiest sales but the least personally rewarding.

Five vacuums were a lot in one day. Our commission was twenty percent, so it made me happy. I think I was smiling when Donna saw me toward the end of the day and maybe she thought I was smiling at her because then she came up right beside me.

"So when are we going to go out," she said, "on a real date?"

"I hadn't really thought about it," I said, but then I saw her face turn ugly and sad and I added, "but it sounds like a good idea," and it changed back to how it was before.

"Where should we go?" she asked.

I didn't know much about these things so I said we could go wherever she liked. I'd dated some girls in college and achieved it when I could, but those relationships usually didn't last very long, and it was never all that important to me anyway since I could achieve it on my own. Mostly I just went to class and read my books and wrote my tests.

"How about the new Italian place?"

"Sure," I said. I knew the one she was talking about.

Her face was bright and she was smiling.

"Friday?"

I nodded.

"Meet you there at seven, then?"

"Seven," I said. I was trying to remember when I'd last gone to an Italian restaurant with a girl but I couldn't. Then I tried to remember the last time I went to any restaurant with a girl and I couldn't. The fact that I couldn't remember made me want to laugh really loud, so I did. I saw a strange look in the faces of a few of my colleagues but Donna just smiled.

"What's so funny?" she asked.

"I was just thinking of something funny," I said.

"I like it," she said.

"What's that?"

"The way you laugh. You should laugh more. It's cute."

"I suppose maybe I should," I said.

She apparently found this funny because she began laughing herself, though on this occasion none of my colleagues looked over with any strange looks on their faces.

"I can hardly wait for Friday," she said.

"Neither can I," I said. And it was true. I had heard many good things about the new Italian restaurant. I had also heard that it was a bit expensive, and I was more thankful than ever that I'd sold the five vacuums.

℘℘℘

I made it home that night at a decent hour and ran into the landlord on the way into the building. He nodded politely at me as I came in and I could tell that he'd completely forgotten about what had happened the night before. My rent check had cleared that day, so I concluded that he must have found the check or realized his error. Either way I was happy that the matter was dealt with. I did feel that he owed me an apology, but then I figured that it wasn't absolutely necessary and thought nothing of it again.

When I took Molly out for her walk that night I

thought about Donna and the new Italian restaurant and the five vacuums I'd sold that day. I also thought that if our date went well and I paid for dinner that maybe she'd come back to my apartment and help me to achieve it.

CHAPTER 7

On Friday I managed to get out of work a few minutes early so I would have time to get home to take Molly out for a nice walk to make sure there wouldn't be a surprise on the kitchen floor that night if Donna decided to come back with me, only I took too much time with Molly and by the time I'd showered and changed and gotten into my car it was already three minutes past seven.

I drove as fast as I could to the new Italian restaurant but must have driven too fast because I was only halfway there when the red lights went up behind me. I pulled over to the right shoulder as I was taught to do in driver's ed.

The officer came up on my driver's side door and

motioned for me to lower my window, which I did. He asked me for my driver's license and I provided him with my new driver's license that I'd just received in the mail that week.

"Do you know how fast you were traveling, sir?"

"No," I answered, though I figured I was probably going pretty fast.

"Do you know what the posted speed limit is on this street?" he asked.

Again I said no, and he didn't ask me anything further. Instead he just told me to wait there and then returned to his cruiser. I saw that the time was now 7:10 and I knew that Donna would be wondering where I was. I figured I should tell him this, so I stepped out of my vehicle, but something about this seemed to upset the officer and he yelled at me to return to my seat, so I did.

I waited there for more than five minutes and I was rather angry by the time he returned to my driver's side window.

"Sir, you were traveling well in excess of the legal limit."

"I'm late for dinner," I said.

"That's no excuse for speeding," said the officer.

"It's not an excuse," I said, "but it's the reason."

"It's not a good reason," said the officer.

He wasn't much of an officer. He was too fat for his uniform, he asked a lot of unnecessary questions, and I could see some sort of mustard stain on his shirt that he'd tried to wipe clean. I suppose it could have been something other than mustard, but I didn't suppose it enough to really believe it.

"Donna is waiting for me at the new Italian restaurant," I said.

The officer just stared at me when I said this and with every second that passed I could imagine Donna wondering where I was and becoming angry with me and felt that it was reducing the chance she might help me to achieve it that night and I could feel myself growing more and more angry. I watched the fat officer tapping my driver's license against his leg like Mr. Peters had tapped my cubicle and something about the sound made my thoughts go wild and by the seventh tap I was gripping the steering wheel with both hands and I'd started to imagine the officer red and open. I thought of getting out of my seat and how he'd probably yell at me to sit back down just as he had before but then before he could react I'd punch him hard in the side of his fat face and knock him to the ground where I'd kick him and kick him and kick him until my foot split his skin and his ribs were all broken and shattered and he was begging and screaming throughout until he fell unconscious from the pain and the loss of blood and how bystanders would have to pull me from him to stop me from killing him if I hadn't killed him already.

"Sir?"

I decided not to do it because I knew he didn't deserve it and because I'd already started into my breathing exercises and was trying to imagine the consequences. That's when I looked at my knuckles and saw how tight they were wrapped around the steering wheel and I wondered where the blood around my knuckles had gone and wondered if the same blood stayed close by the knuckles waiting to go back to where it came from or if it just ran off and mixed with the rest of my body only to be replaced by new blood and then finally the officer's voice drew back my attention.

"Yes?" I said.

"Are you all right, sir?"

"Yes," I said. I'd considered telling him that I was angry, but then I figured he might ask more questions and that would make me even later than I already was.

Finally he handed back my driver's license and the ticket that he'd written that amounted to the commission I would receive on more than three vacuums and told me to "slow down," which was a silly thing to say since I wasn't even moving, but then I realized he must have meant when I started driving again and I was going to tell him "Okay," but by then he'd already walked away.

I drove the speed limit the remainder of the way to the restaurant and was quite late by the time I'd parked and walked into the front entrance.

"Can I help you?"

The greeter was a thin young girl of maybe eighteen. I told her that I was looking for Donna and she said that she didn't know who that was so then I told her that I was supposed to meet a lady here at seven and she told me that it was seven-thirty and I told her that I knew that but before either of us could say anything more I could see Donna seated in the restaurant so I just walked over to where she was sitting and took a seat in the chair across from her.

Donna had a look on her face not unlike the officer when he was tapping my driver's license against his leg. She was cradling a glass of wine that was nearly empty.

"Would you like some more wine?" I asked.

She didn't answer. I figured this meant that either she didn't want to talk to me because I was late or else she didn't have much to say.

I was hoping it was that she didn't have much to say but either way I figured it would be best not to press her, so I started looking through the menu, only there must have been something about this that changed her mind because then she started to talk.

"Do you know how long I've been here?" she asked.

"Probably thirty minutes," I said.

"Longer," she said. "I got here early."

There were tears in her eyes so I put down the menu.

"Do you even want to be here tonight?" she asked.

I said that I did and then explained that I'd walked Molly too long and then had to speed and how I was stopped by the fat police officer with the mustard-stained shirt. I didn't mention how angry I'd gotten or some of the other things I'd been thinking because my parents had taught me that stuff didn't make for good conversation with most people except for them and my counselors.

"I'm sorry I'm late," I said, and it was true. I'd been looking forward to coming to this restaurant and by then I was very hungry. This seemed to calm her, and she smiled for the first time that night.

We had some wine and before long we'd ordered our meals. I selected something cheaper than what I'd really wanted because I couldn't help thinking about the speed-ing ticket that equaled more than three vacuums worth of commission.

"So what do you like to do," she asked, "when you're not working or walking your dog or watching TV?"

I thought about it, but there really wasn't much be-yond those things so I asked her about what she liked to do.

"Well, you're going to think this is silly but I play the viola," she said.

"What is that?" I asked.

"It's basically a violin but smaller."

"I guess that makes sense."

"I've played it since I was little. I'm pretty good at it."

"I bet you are," I said.

She sipped her wine and smiled as the glass was at her mouth.

"You think I'm ridiculous," she said.

"Not at all."

"Then what are you thinking?"

"Now?"

"Right now," she said.

What I was actually thinking about were her breasts, which were half peeking out above her blouse, but I figured I shouldn't mention it, so I lied and told her I was thinking about my dog.

"You like animals, don't you?"

"Very much," I said. "My family had animals, and I spent a lot of time with them when I was young."

"What kinds of animals?"

"Dogs, rabbits. We had some hamsters, too."

"No cats?"

"Cats are strange creatures," I said. "I don't trust them altogether."

She laughed.

"Well, even without cats, that's still a lot of animals," she said.

I said she was right because it probably was a lot of animals. My parents always seemed to keep animals around ever since one of my counselors suggested it was good for me. When I moved away from home, it was hard not to have their company, so I bought two hamsters, but they didn't live very long and then I didn't have another animal until Molly.

"Have you always had one? A dog, I mean?"

"Not always. I went away to college and they don't like dogs on campus," I said, and this was true. "Then I started to work and lived alone and didn't know if I could take care of an animal and work."

"So then how'd you end up with Molly?" she asked.

Like my angry thoughts about the fat officer and my thoughts about her breasts, I figured I shouldn't really talk about it, so I made up something else and it must have sounded good because she laughed and then our food arrived not long after.

"Have you always liked animals?"

"Yes," I said, and that was true, too, but it wasn't really the whole truth. My parents liked me to have animals around. They told me that it made me calm when they were around and maybe they were right. I'd attacked a boy at school for throwing rocks at a bird, and the teacher said that what I'd done to him they hadn't seen before because I'd poked him right in the eye with a stick and I heard he needed surgeries for the eye and I never saw him back at my school again.

"So what makes you such an animal lover?"

I wanted to tell her that it calmed me and about what happened at school when I was young, but instead I just said because they were furry and warm, and she laughed at that and then sipped her wine again to make her glass empty.

My food was really good and I was glad that I hadn't ordered the more expensive item that I probably would have ordered if the fat police officer with the mustard stain hadn't given me the ticket that I surely deserved because I couldn't imagine enjoying it any more than what I was eating now, so there would really have been no point in spending the extra money. I asked Donna how her food was and she said it was perfect. I hadn't had a chance to see how much her meal would cost before they took the menus away but from the looks of things and the smile on her face I figured it would probably cost at least the commission of one and a half vacuums.

"You really don't talk all that much do you?" she asked.

"Not so much," I said. I started to think that maybe she was slow because she asked a lot of questions that had obvious answers, then I felt bad for thinking she was slow and before I realized it, I'd said sorry.

"What are you apologizing for?"

"For being late," I said, and she seemed to accept this.

"I think some of the guys at work like you," I said.

"Mm-hmm? Which ones?"

"Jeff for sure," I said.

"He's a creep," she said, and I agreed.

"Who else?"

"Gary, I think."

"Too old," she said.

I nodded.

"And too married," she added, then laughed and reached out to put her hand around mine. "Anyway, is someone getting a little jealous?"

She wriggled her face up into a smile and started to rub my arm. I told her I wasn't jealous at all, but she must have figured I was joking or playing coy because she started to laugh, and then I decided to laugh along with her.

It was getting late by the time she ordered dessert. I had a coffee because I was starting to get tired, but I was still hoping to stay up later and see if she'd help me to achieve it. When we finally left the restaurant it was almost eleven o'clock. I hadn't had too much to drink and suggested that I could drive us home.

I drove her to my apartment and before long her blouse was on my bedroom floor and she'd helped me to achieve it. Again she didn't seem to mind that it finished so quickly because she curled up by my side and I could see a contented look on her face even though her eyes were closed.

"What are you thinking about?" she said after a minute or two.

The fact was that I was thinking about how the commission from the five vacuums would have been all used up because of the speeding ticket and the dinner, but instead I told her that I was thinking about her and that seemed to be a good answer because she hugged me closer and went to sleep, and it let me go back to my thinking.

CHAPTER 8

Donna called Sunday night and didn't seem happy, and she asked me why I hadn't called her since she left my apartment on Saturday morning. I told her that I didn't like talking on the telephone, and she told me I needed to "Get with the times," but at least then she stopped being mad at me, and we talked for a bit before I took Molly for a walk and watched some television.

I was at work early on Monday when Mr. Peters called me into his office. He was the only one of us who had a real office with walls and a ceiling and a door that could close. He had me sit in a chair opposite his desk and once we were both seated he looked at me in a curious way but didn't say anything. Finally, he asked me if I was involved with Donna, and though he didn't actually use the words "intercourse" or "sex," I was fairly certain that was what he was talking about.

It made me think about how Donna had helped me to achieve it several times, but I didn't want to answer his question so I didn't. Instead, I thought about how Mr. Peters would have come to know about it in the first place and figured maybe Jeff or Gary had told him because they were jealous, but then I realized Jeff and Gary wouldn't know for sure what was going on in my bedroom and maybe they hadn't said anything at all and so I immediately felt bad for disparaging them in my mind.

"Well?" he said.

"I've spent some time with her," I said. "We went to that new Italian restaurant." I told him what I'd ordered, but he didn't seem very interested in that.

He sort of sat up in his seat and changed his expression. Maybe a bit more friendly, though I wouldn't have said it was all the way friendly.

"Let me ask you a question," he said. "Have you ever heard the saying that you shouldn't dip your pen in company ink?"

"No," I said.

He shifted again in his seat.

"Well, let's put it another way. Work relationships can complicate things."

"I suppose," I said.

"Don't get me wrong. Ms. Wintergrass is a lovely young woman."

When he first said "Ms. Wintergrass," I didn't know who he was talking about but then a second later I realized that he was talking about Donna. I really only considered her "Donna" and had never considered her last name. I then wondered if this made me inconsiderate, but then I figured that even if it had been inconsiderate that I was no longer so because I'd now considered it.

"Yes," is all I said.

"She's a little younger than you, of course. Not that that means too much these days. But you probably know that our company frowns on fraternizing within the ranks."

"I didn't know that."

"Well, it's not exactly in the rule book," said Mr. Peters. "But Ms. Wintergrass isn't a salesperson. She takes phone calls and processes orders and what would stop her from sending a few sales in your direction if she liked you in a special way?"

I hadn't really thought about that.

"I suppose that might not be fair," I said.

"No, you see now, don't you?"

"But I've always sold well," I said, "even before we went to the new Italian restaurant."

He smiled at this.

"Yes, you have. You're consistently one of my top

salesmen. It's pretty incredible. I've listened to some of your sales pitches. You have a very different style, don't you? Very simple and straightforward. Very direct."

There was something in his voice that sounded as if he was surprised that I was able to sell so many vacuums.

"'Assault them with honesty,'" I said.

He leaned back in his chair and smiled when I said it. "Assault Them with Honesty" was the sixth rule of *The Company Culture Handbook.*

"Well, whatever you're doing, keep it up—at least as far as the vacuum sales go."

"I will," I said.

"You get what I'm saying, right?"

"Yes," I said and left his office to start my work.

Donna soon arrived at her cubicle, but not before stopping beside me and touching me on my shoulder. I tried to ignore her since I'd just had the discussion with Mr. Peters, but it was hard to ignore her, given the way she was acting and the blouse she was wearing, which was one of the two blouses that had been left on my bedroom floor while she helped me to achieve it.

"We should talk," I said.

Her body language changed drastically when I said this and she said we should talk right now but I told her I couldn't because I had to call back Mrs. Ranger about her order, but then Donna said "Fuck Mrs. Ranger" and though I didn't feel that her response was entirely called for, I did hold off making the phone call.

"I had a meeting with Mr. Peters this morning," I said.

She seemed to be waiting for me to say more so I continued.

"He heard we were spending time together and told me that the company frowns on fraternizing within the ranks."

"Fraternizing within the ranks," she repeated rather coldly.

"I think it means—"

"I know what it means," she said.

I then thought maybe I could call Mrs. Ranger, but when I picked up the receiver Donna kept talking.

"So what did he say, exactly? Did he tell you to stop seeing me?"

"No," I said. "He didn't say that exactly."

"All right, then." And she squeezed my shoulder and returned to her cubicle.

The rest of the day went by without incident and I sold four vacuums and resolved Mrs. Ranger's problem, so all in all it was a good day.

CHAPTER 9

I got home and took Molly for a walk and then had dinner and took the garbage outside to the back dumpster. The landlord was out back raking leaves and I could see that he'd chained his dog to the back fence and the dog was shivering. The dog was skinny and had a dull coat and I thought that maybe it was even mangy, but then I felt bad for thinking that and it made me want to apologize to the dog but then he wouldn't understand me even if I did so I figured there'd be no point.

I walked closer to them by pretending I was just taking a walk around the grounds and as I got closer it seemed as if one of the dog's legs was hurt because it was bent at a strange angle, so I asked the landlord what had happened. He stopped raking the leaves and brushed his shirtsleeve across his forehead to wipe away some of the sweat that had collected.

"Dog is always running into things," he said.

"What did he run into?" I asked.

"How the hell am I supposed to know?" he said then resumed raking the leaves.

"I think maybe he needs to go to the veterinarian," I said.

"You do, do you?"

"I do."

"And you gonna pay for it?"

"I don't see why I should have to pay for it," I said, and when he didn't say anything further, I just went back inside my apartment and to my own dog who also sometimes ran into things but who'd never ended up with a crooked leg.

☙☙☙

I took Molly for another walk just before bedtime which is something I usually did, and when we left through the front lobby I could hear the landlord's dog barking through his door, and then I heard it yelp as if it had been grabbed or hit and the barking stopped quickly, and then I continued on out the door with Molly.

I took her on an extra-long walk and after a while I couldn't feel my hand anymore, and I thought maybe it was just because of the cool air, but then I realized I'd been clenching the leash so tight that it had cut the blood off from my fingers, so I loosened my grip and let the blood go back to where it belonged.

When we got back inside, I stopped beside the landlord's door and tried to listen for any noises coming from his apartment, but I couldn't hear any except maybe the television, so I went back upstairs and turned on my own television and watched a show, but it wasn't much of a show, so I turned it off and soon fell asleep.

CHAPTER 10

The rest of the week went by without incident. Mr. Peters left me alone and Donna seemed to make some effort at not fraternizing, though she did still send me suggestive looks whenever she could and I could tell that she was still interested in helping me to achieve it, which pleased me. I also sold almost twenty vacuums that week which was a good haul and helped make up for the speeding ticket and the restaurant bill.

On Friday Donna asked me what I was doing that weekend and I said that I hadn't much thought about it and she must have thought I was being coy again because she smiled and said "I bet you haven't" and touched me on my arm.

Then she asked if I wanted to meet at a bar that night

and I told her there was a bar close to my place and we agreed to meet there at eight.

I went home and took Molly for a walk and saw the landlord outside raking leaves again but didn't see his dog anywhere, so I just went inside where I saw one of the older tenants who lived in my building and she commented on Molly being "a good little dog" and I said that she was indeed a good dog. I then asked her if she'd seen the landlord's dog, and she told me that the landlord's dog had died. I asked her how it had died and she said that she didn't know, but that the landlord had told her it had some health issues. The whole thing made me think of the incident two years ago and though I was listening to the old lady I was also practicing the breathing exercises that I'd been taught that were meant to slow down my thinking and help me to control some of the scary thoughts that sometimes went through my head.

Once back in my apartment I thought about the landlord's dog and Molly and the incident and I no longer felt like going out to the bar, but then I'd already told Donna I would be there, so I felt that I shouldn't cancel and that maybe if I continued on with my breathing exercises and had some drinks and if she helped me to achieve it, then I'd probably feel better than I did at that moment.

CHAPTER 11

I got there early to make up for being late to the restaurant last week and once she arrived we took a booth near the back of the pub and ordered some beer and we each took a few sips in silence.

"Why are you always so quiet?" she asked.

I wanted to tell her that I was only quiet with my words and that I was usually loud in my mind, but instead I just told her that there wasn't much to say most of the time.

"Maybe that's why I like you so much," she said. "You're not always blabbing away like so many guys do. It's so refreshing."

"That's good," I said.

"What are we going to do about Peters?" she asked.

"What's to be done?" is all I said.

"I don't think it's any of their business," she said.

"He thinks you will give me preferential treatment."

"I don't see how I could."

"He seems to think it's possible."

"I wonder if I should talk to him?"

"I'm not sure," I said. "You can if you want to."

"Do you want me to?"

"It doesn't matter to me," I said.

After I said this she pulled away from me and turned sort of rigid. She then asked me if I liked her and I told her that I did.

It was clear that Donna was self-conscious about whether I liked her or not. The funny thing about women was that the more self-conscious they were about if you liked them, the more they seemed to like you in return, which didn't seem to make much sense because you would think they'd be better off liking boys that clearly liked them back.

"Why do you like me?" she said.

I told her that she was always nice to me and when I said I also liked her blouses, her cheeks went red to match the color of the blouse she'd worn that night.

I asked her if she liked me, even though I knew that she did because she was always touching me and wanting me to call her and helping me to achieve it and not caring about how long it took me when I did.

"Isn't it obvious?" she said then cozied back up to me and kissed my cheek.

"I suppose it is."

"So then why don't you care if I talk to him?"

"I just mean it's your decision to do so."

"What will you do if he tells us to stop seeing each other?"

"I haven't thought about it," I said then took another sip of beer.

Again she pulled away from my shoulder and became rigid. She apparently did so each time I gave her a response that she didn't like, but then I figured I should tell the truth whenever possible, even if it meant that she would do that.

"So it doesn't matter either way to you, does it?"

I told her that it did matter, but that my job was important and I couldn't risk it, no matter how much I liked her blouses, and she smiled and came back to my side. I had often found that women could change between angry and happy very quickly, but it seemed especially true with Donna.

We got back to my place close to midnight and as we walked through the front lobby I stopped by the landlord's door to listen and I could hear him laughing at something on the television set. Donna asked me what I was doing and I just told her that I thought I heard something and then went up with her in the elevator.

Once inside my apartment I wanted to see her red blouse on the floor but she wanted to keep drinking, so I took some beer out of my fridge and placed it on the counter. Molly was excited to see us and was running around our feet. I found that I'd been drinking more often since I'd started seeing Donna and I wasn't sure it was such a good idea because it became harder to control my thoughts and the breathing exercises didn't always work so well but then there hadn't been an incident for nearly two years so I figured it would be okay.

We each had two more beers and when Donna got up to get a third Molly ran out to greet her and Donna stepped on one of her paws and Molly let out a wild yelp and I shot up from my seat as fast as I could, given my impaired condition, and immediately thought of Donna as red and open.

Donna bent over Molly and apologized to her but nearly fell over when she did because she was so unsteady on her feet because of all the alcohol. Molly ran back several steps and whimpered and I looked at Donna very angrily and I saw her look at me and she seemed scared and I tried my breathing exercises but the beer got in the way so I said *not her fault* in my mind and closed my eyes.

Not her fault.
Not her fault.
Not her fault.

Not her fault.
Not her fault.
Not her fault.

I felt an arm on mine and opened my eyes and saw Donna's face and she seemed to be crying and it made it easier for the thoughts to go away and then she hugged me and we kissed and soon after we were in the bedroom with her blouse on the floor and both of us naked and she helped me to achieve it and as she curled up against me afterward I felt guilty for ever thinking of her as red and open.

CHAPTER 12

Donna went home the next morning but we agreed to meet that night at eight o'clock which would be the first time we'd met on consecutive nights and the first time I'd seen a girl on consecutive nights since college.

Molly was fine and was walking normally by then so it seemed as if she might have just overreacted to what had happened or perhaps had a low threshold for pain. Either way, I took her for a long walk and the air made me feel better, and I spent the rest of the day reviewing some orders before I went to make dinner, but I didn't get very far because the faucet stopped working altogether and I needed water to make my dinner.

I went down to the first floor and knocked on the

landlord's door. He didn't immediately answer but after I knocked a second time the door swept open and he was standing in shorts and a thin white T-shirt.

"Yeah?"

"My sink," I said.

"What about it?"

"Remember how I told you it was broken?"

He seemed to think it over but then told me he didn't know what I was talking about.

"It's stopped working," I said.

"You can fill out a work order," he said, motioning toward a box that was to the right of his door and had some white pieces of paper sticking out of it and a pencil on a thin ledge at the bottom.

"I need water to make my dinner," I said.

"You still got water from the bathroom faucets?" he asked.

"I suppose so," I said. "But then that's bathroom water and it would be difficult to make dinner with that."

The landlord looked at me queerly and shook his head but finally told me he'd look for his tools.

He left the door open and I stepped a foot inside and could see a large unchewed dog bone on the floor along with some other junk. The landlord returned after a few minutes and he'd changed his shirt but was still wearing his shorts.

He put on a pair of sandals and followed me upstairs

to my apartment where I took him to the sink where the faucet didn't work. Molly kept a safe distance back from him as he bent down and started pulling some of the junk from beneath the sink including the pail that had been catching the leaky water and was now practically overflowing.

He asked me for the flashlight so I leaned over and handed it to him and then his head and shoulders disappeared beneath my sink and I heard him muttering this thing or that but I still felt a bit wobbly from all the beer the prior night and placed a hand on my counter for balance.

I heard him tugging at the pipes and then swear a few times and it made me think of how he used to talk to his dog and I thought of the dog's crooked leg and the mostly un-chewed bone in the landlord's entryway and I started into my breathing exercises but they didn't seem to help so when he asked me to pass him his wrench all I could think of was seeing him red and open and it made me want to pick up the wrench from his toolbox and smash it into his skull over and over and over again until his skull was smashed in and the blood was pouring free and open from where I'd caved his head in and how Molly would be barking at my feet and not understanding what was happening but how I wouldn't stop until he was still and lifeless and red and open.

I was thinking of all this when he asked me again for the wrench.

And then I did what I was thinking.

CHAPTER 13

It took me several hours to clean it up.

I briefly felt bad about what I'd done, but then I knew what he must have done to his dog, so I didn't feel bad for very long. I did regret not letting him fix my sink before I did it, but then I was swept up by my emotions so it couldn't be helped.

I had to pull him into my bathtub and clean myself up well enough to go find a hacksaw and there was blood everywhere. It all washed up well enough with some soap and bleach, but I was exhausted by the time I was supposed to meet Donna. I thought that perhaps I should cancel but then I couldn't think of a good excuse to get out of it so I just decided to go. I did call her and ask if we could push it back to nine and so we met at a bar by her place and had some beers and went back to her place for the first time.

She had a small apartment that was a bit smaller than my own and a pet turtle named Bob and not a lot of furniture. She opened a bottle of wine that we shared and nearly finished and we talked about this or that but she did most of the talking because I was thinking about this second incident that had now happened and how most of the landlord was in garbage bags in my closet and wondering how I would dispose of them in a way that wouldn't smell or draw the attention of raccoons or other animals that might open the bags so I thought Donna might be able to help.

"I need to get rid of something," I said.

"Oh yeah?" she smiled. "Hopefully you're not talking about me?"

I laughed my loud laugh that sometimes had some of my colleagues staring at me but it felt really good to laugh at that moment and it made me feel better once I had finished.

"I like it when you laugh," she said. "I wish you'd laugh more often."

"I guess I could, but then maybe it's better when I do finally laugh because then it makes it more special."

"Maybe you're right," she said, then laughed herself before asking me what I needed to get rid of, and whatever I was going to say I'd already forgotten in our discussion about the laughing, but I knew I couldn't say it was garbage bags with my landlord inside so I said nothing. But then she pressed me so I told her I wanted to get rid of my green chair and as soon as I said that she got excited and asked if she could have it instead and I felt as if I had no choice so I said that she could have it even though it was actually my favorite chair.

"But I don't have a car so can you bring it to me somehow?"

"It won't fit in my car," I said, and I thought that maybe that would save my green chair, but then she said she had a friend with a truck so that it would be okay and I agreed again to give her the chair.

"But where would you get rid of a chair like that if you wanted to?" I asked.

"I don't know. The dump maybe."

"The dump," I repeated.

"Why do you want to get rid of it? It's so comfortable."

She was right, it was very comfortable, and I almost rescinded my offer of the chair, but then I figured that would bring a lot of other uncomfortable questions, so I just said that it was old and I was thinking of getting a new chair. Then she asked if I wanted to keep it until I actually bought a new one, and I thought that was a perfectly good excuse to hold onto the chair a bit longer so I agreed. I was also thinking of the dump and thought that it would be a good place to dispose of the landlord as long as I could get the garbage bags into my trunk without bringing too much suspicion on me.

That night was the first night she helped me to achieve it at her place, and though she wasn't wearing a blouse, the dress she had on looked good on the bedroom floor, and I had a great night of sleep because Bob the turtle didn't wake us up early like Molly always did, and he didn't even need to be taken for a walk.

CHAPTER 14

I got home early Sunday and took Molly for a walk and when I got back inside I saw the same old lady tenant at the landlord's door.

"Have you seen him around?" she asked.

"Not since yesterday," I said.

"He was supposed to help me with something," she said.

I nodded because I didn't know what else to say.

"It's the darndest thing," she said. "I think I can hear the TV inside but nobody answers."

"Maybe he's asleep," I said.

The woman didn't say anything else, so Molly and I took the elevator back up to my apartment.

Later on I did a test-run to the back parking lot with

a box of rubbish and placed it in my trunk. It was late and there wasn't anybody else back there, so I returned with two of the bags and placed them into the trunk then went back up and returned with the final two bags and drove quickly to the dump, where I discarded the bags in something of a landfill and did the same with his toolbox.

By Tuesday the owner of the building had come around looking for the landlord and had apparently called the police because when I got home from work that day I saw his apartment door open and the owner was speaking with an officer just inside the front entryway, where I could still see the un-chewed dog bone.

I nodded to the officer and went up the elevator to get Molly and then took her out for her walk. As we returned through the lobby, there was a second officer along with the first, and he asked if he could take a statement from me and I said that would be fine, and I asked him if he would like to come up to my apartment, but he said that wouldn't be necessary and that he could take the statement right there in the entryway.

"Sir, could you give me your name and address?"

I provided them easily.

"Could you tell me the last time you saw the landlord?"

"This weekend. I asked him to fix my sink."

"When exactly was this?"

"I think it was Friday or Saturday."

"Can you be any more precise, sir?"

"Saturday then," I said.

"Can you tell me what time that was?"

"I think it was daytime. Maybe close to dinner."

It made me hungry to think about it because I'd been so hungry when I'd gone to him to ask him to fix my sink, and I really had no thoughts of killing him when I went there and was only thinking of getting my faucet fixed so I could make some dinner and then what happened had happened and I hadn't been able to eat until I met up with Donna at the bar close to her apartment at nine.

"Have you seen anyone around here who looked suspicious or looked like they didn't belong?"

To me those seemed like they were two different things but still I answered no to both.

"Did you know him well?"

"Not very."

"One of the neighbors said he had a dog. Have you seen the dog around?"

"I heard the dog died," I said.

The officer didn't say anything but just scratched some words down on his notepad.

"What sort of a relationship did you have with him?"

"I didn't know him that well. He liked to drink a lot."

"I see," said the officer.

"My sink still needs to be fixed," I said and then ex-

plained that no water came out of the faucet and that I
had been forced to get my water from the bathroom sink
and that it didn't seem right to make dinner with water
from the bathroom.

The officer just nodded but didn't write anything
down. He took my phone number, and finally Molly and I
stepped back into the elevator and as the doors closed I
could still see him scribbling things in his notebook and
looking in our direction.

CHAPTER 15

By Thursday he had been reported in the newspaper as a missing person.

"Isn't that your building?" asked Donna when she saw me reading the story.

"Yes."

"Crazy," she said.

"Yes."

"What do you think happened to him?"

"Could have been a lot of things. He drank a lot." It didn't bother me to say these things because both of them were true.

"Are you scared?"

"Why should I be?"

"I guess you shouldn't."

She'd taken my hand in her own and it made me uncomfortable because Mr. Peters was floating around and Donna had already put two lay-downs through to my line that day.

"The police asked me some questions," I said.

Donna looked at me as if with suspicion, though maybe it was just concern.

"Why were they talking to you?"

"I suppose they were talking to everyone in the building," I said, and her look of concern or suspicion mostly went away.

I could see Mr. Peters staring at us, so I told Donna she should probably get back to her own cubicle and so she did but only after another minute of chatting, then I spent the rest of the day making calls and sold three vacuums, which wasn't too bad, especially when considering that my mind was mostly occupied with what had happened on Saturday.

Donna called me later that night and asked if I'd like to meet her for a drink and I said I didn't want to because I was tired although the real reason was that I just didn't want to, but then she asked me again and hinted that she'd probably help me to achieve it, and I decided that maybe I wanted to go after all, so I got dressed and left my apartment.

I was stepping out of my building when I saw the same police officer who'd taken my statement. He was speaking to another tenant of my building on the sidewalk by his police cruiser, but when he saw me his face changed, and I saw him say something quickly to the man he'd been talking to, and then he walked briskly in my direction.

"Sir…"

I figured he was probably talking to me, but I ignored him and kept walking toward the side of the building where I parked my car.

"Sir, if I could have a word with you…"

He'd caught up to me sufficiently that I felt I couldn't ignore him any longer, so I stopped and turned around and asked him if he was talking to me, and he said that he was so I asked him what he wanted.

"Do you remember talking to me earlier this week, in the lobby?"

I told him that I remembered. He didn't say anything after that and so it seemed as if maybe that was his only question, so I started to walk away but then he called for me again.

"You in a hurry to get somewhere?" He said it with a sharper tone than he'd used before.

"I'm going to see Donna," I said.

"Who's that?"

"A girl I date. We went to the new Italian restaurant. Have you been?"

The officer shook his head.

"I'm supposed to meet her now," I added.

"I see. Well, if you could just spare a few minutes?"

I told him that I could.

"I just wanted to ask you about something, about your dog…"

"Molly," I said.

"Yes, well about that. How long would you say that you've had Molly?"

I told him that I'd had Molly for close to two years.

"I see."

He removed his notepad from his pocket and scribbled something down in it, presumably that I'd had Molly for two years since that was what I had just said, but then I suppose he could have written something else about me, or something different altogether, like what he might like for supper tomorrow.

"Would you mind telling me where you got her?" he asked.

I told him that I'd found her in the street. That she was cold and hungry and I fed her and that she followed me home and that I decided to take care of her and took her to the veterinarian to get her shots and that I named her Molly, but for all I knew Molly wasn't her real name, but how it would have been a nice coincidence if it actually was her name, and probably a coincidence that Molly would have appreciated.

The officer just looked at me and didn't say anything

except "I see," which seemed to be something he liked to say.

"Can you tell me exactly where you found her?"

I thought it over for a moment then answered, "Not much more than four or five blocks from here—in that direction."

After I pointed, he scribbled something else in his notepad and again said, "I see."

"There are too many stray dogs," I said. "It's not safe or sanitary for us or for the dogs themselves."

He said, "I see" once again but didn't scribble anything down that time.

"What kind of a dog is it?"

"The veterinarian told me that she was a Cocker Spaniel mix but didn't tell me what she was mixed with."

More scribbling.

"She's a pretty good dog, only sometimes she'll leave me a surprise on the kitchen floor if I don't get home in time to walk her."

No scribbling.

The officer paused at that moment and I considered walking away again, only it seemed as if he wanted to say something else, and eventually he did.

"Sir, if I say the name 'Sherman Dempsey,' does that mean anything to you?"

I told him that it didn't. He just stared at me for a few seconds after that as if he was trying to read my face or perhaps hoping that my answer would change, but I couldn't change my answer because it was the truth.

"Mr. Dempsey died not too far from here. Reports are that he had a brown Cocker Spaniel."

"I see," I said, then I laughed because I realized I'd just said the same two words the officer had kept saying, and I must have laughed very loud because the officer looked at me rather suspiciously, just like Donna had looked at me when I told her that the police had been questioning me, only with the officer there was no concern mixed in.

"Is something funny, sir?"

I explained what it was, but he didn't seem to think it was as funny as I did because he didn't laugh at all.

"Do you think Molly is Mr. Dempsey's dog?" I asked.

"Possibly," he responded.

"Do you think there might be a reward in it for me?" I said.

"A reward?" asked the officer.

"Yes, because I found the missing dog."

"The owner of the dog is dead, sir."

"Yes," I said, "but maybe there still might be some reward to be had."

"Mr. Dempsey was murdered, sir. Not more than six blocks from here."

"I see," I said then managed to keep from laughing,

even though I had a great urge to do so.

"You wouldn't know anything about that would you, son?"

He wasn't much older than me so I found it odd he would call me "son."

"How could I possibly?" I said.

One of the things we learned when we sold vacuums was to turn the conversation around and put the other person on the defensive with a question when necessary. This was the eighth rule of *The Company Culture Handbook:* "Control the Conversation."

The officer didn't answer, but then he also didn't ask me any further questions, so I figured I'd controlled the conversation about as well as I could have. I then told him I had to leave or else Donna would be mad at me and I went to my car and drove away.

CHAPTER 16

The first rule of *The Company Culture Handbook* is to "Always Stay Positive." By this they meant that you should always remain upbeat and that good things will inevitably flow from this, so on the ride over I tried to think of all the good things in my life like Molly and my apartment and my job and how Donna had been helping me to achieve it on a regular basis, but no matter how hard I tried I still couldn't help thinking about the first incident and how I'd found the man in the alley and how that man must have been Sherman Dempsey because it would have been too big of a coincidence for another man to have been killed six blocks from my apartment who also happened to have a brown Cocker Spaniel.

When I'd told the officer that the name Sherman

Dempsey didn't mean anything to me it was the truth because it didn't mean anything to me when he first said it. If he had asked me again after I'd made the connection then it would have been a lie for me to say it didn't mean anything to me, but he didn't ask me again so I was happy not to have had to lie to the officer.

The incident was two years earlier, and I remember the time very well because I'd sold twenty vacuums to a company earlier that week and on Friday when I received my paycheck it was the biggest one that I'd ever seen.

I'd gone out to celebrate and sat at a bar and shared my story and people seemed genuinely interested in my sale of the twenty vacuums.

I also kept buying their drinks, but I think they would have wanted to hear about the vacuums all the same. I don't remember how many beers I had that night but I do remember that it was a lot more than normal and that I had to leave my car there and take a taxi or else walk home, and I remember feeling so good and the weather being so nice that I decided to walk home and so I did.

The streets were mostly deserted as I got closer to my neighborhood and it was quiet too, so when I walked past the alleyway I could easily hear the noises that were coming from inside so I staggered into the alley and found the man who I now know to be Sherman Dempsey and I saw him beating on Molly, though her name may not have been Molly back then.

I remember how he was yelling at her and how he was punching her in the side of her head and how Molly would sometimes yelp and sometimes growl but mostly how she just shook and curled. I remember stepping farther into the alley and asking the man what he was doing, but the man just told me to mind my own business and used some words that I don't much like repeating and I remember that was when I knew that I needed to make him red and open.

I was still wearing my best suit which was my blue pin-stripe one, and even though we didn't come face-to-face with many customers unless we worked in the retail locations, the fourth rule of *The Company Culture Handbook* was "Dress the Part," which meant that if you wanted to be considered a professional then you should dress like one and smile and stay well-groomed, even if the customers couldn't actually see you.

Sherman Dempsey had started yelling at Molly again with some of the same words that I don't much like repeating, and by the way he was speaking and moving it seemed like he was probably drunk, though perhaps not as drunk as I was.

I felt around in my blue suit for my Swiss army knife with the Polar Bear on the handle that I always carried, and I thought I'd opened up the largest of the two knife options, but only after I'd first flipped out the scissors because I could hardly tell which was which since it was so dark and because I was so drunk. I walked up behind Mr. Dempsey and told him again that he should stop doing what he was doing and again he told me to mind my own business so I stabbed him seventeen times in the neck with the big knife and only realized after the fact that it was the file I'd used and that I'd never actually opened up the big knife at all because it was so dark and because I was so drunk and I remember how I'd wondered if I would have needed to stab him seventeen times if I'd been using the big knife instead of the file but then figured that I would never know the answer for sure.

He'd fallen to the ground after about the fourth or fifth stab so I delivered the rest while he was flailing on the ground next to Molly who was still shaking and curled. I hadn't bothered with any of my breathing exercises at that point because I knew that he had to be red and open or else he might make Molly red and open and I wanted to ensure that never happened, and though maybe there were other ways I could have ensured it, this was the most immediate and the most certain.

After it was over I left him there and I carried Molly back to my apartment and was glad it was so late and we were so close because my suit was covered in blood and it would have been bad if anyone had seen me, but I don't think that anyone did.

I set Molly on the floor and removed all of my clothing and stepped into the shower and by the time I got out

of the shower I could hear banging on my front door
where Molly was howling, so I hurried to put on clothing
and ran to open the door to find the landlord whom I
would later murder with a wrench beneath my sink.

"What the hell is going on in here?"

I was still drunk and slightly shaken by the incident
so I asked him what he was referring to.

"The dog," he said. "The fucking dog is howling at
the door. Do you know what time it is?"

"I do not," I said. I said it because it was true.

"And since when did you get a fucking dog?" he
said.

I didn't much like his attitude, but then it pleased me
that he was interested in the dog so I started to tell him
that I found the dog wandering loose on the way home,
which was mostly the truth, but then he told me he didn't
care where I got the dog and only cared that I keep it quiet and that it not disturb the neighbors.

Once he left I managed to calm Molly down and after a while she stopped shaking and even fell asleep and
then I used some bleach to wash my Swiss army knife
and though I thought maybe I should throw it into a garbage bag with my bloody suit, I also thought that maybe
it would be dumb to put the murder weapon along with
the murder clothes in the same bag, and I also liked that
knife because I'd won it in one of our contests, and even
if it wasn't much of a knife it worked well enough and

had a Polar Bear on the handle so I decided to keep it.

And that was the incident that I thought about on the car ride over to see Donna. I mostly tried not to think of it, but sometimes it couldn't be helped and as it turned out this was one of the sometimes that it couldn't.

CHAPTER 17

I met Donna at a bar called Rodion's which was close
to where she lived and we took up a booth and drank
some beer. She told me that she'd started putting lay-
downs through to my extension when people called in for
vacuums even though they were supposed to go to who-
ever wasn't busy because she'd been insulted that Mr.
Peters had insinuated that she would show favoritism in
my direction. I told her that it might not be good to get
back at the boss by doing exactly what he said she might
do and also told her that the other salesmen might complain and that she might get in trouble.

"It's a shitty job anyway," she said.

"Why do you say that?"

"You've read the company handbook, haven't you?

Such brainwashing company bullshit. 'The Company is Your Friend?' Jesus Christ!"

"The Company is Your Friend" was the tenth and final rule of *The Company Culture Handbook.* I'd actually been rather fond of the company culture up to that point, but then "Nobody Likes a Challenger" was the ninth rule and meant that you shouldn't undermine people's beliefs, no matter how wrong or irrational they might be. We were taught to just agree with them but then later to try to change their view without them actually knowing it, so I didn't say anything more about it to Donna at that time.

We drank some more beer and Donna asked me if I loved her, but I was still thinking of the incident from two years ago and didn't much feel like talking about love so I said I didn't want to talk about it.

Then Donna started to cry, so I figured it was the wrong thing to say, even though it was the truth, so I told her that the subject just made me uncomfortable and she stopped crying a moment later.

"I love you," she said.

"I see."

I thought of how I was still repeating what the police officer kept saying and it made me want to laugh, but I felt it might not be appropriate in the circumstances since she'd just been crying and was now confiding her feelings to me, so I resisted the urge to laugh and instead took a sip of my beer.

"Don't you have anything to say about it?" she said.

"Like what?"

She didn't answer right away and it looked like she might cry again, but she didn't. Donna cried an awful lot and especially when she'd been drinking, and I thought about how we were quite different in that respect because I don't remember crying once in my entire life. I thought this was funny and it made me want to laugh, but then I thought maybe it was sad that I never cried and that depressed me sufficiently enough not to laugh but still not enough to cry, but I thought maybe it would have been ironic if I had.

"Don't I mean anything to you?" said Donna.

"Of course you do."

Then she started to cry again anyway and I thought I'd said something wrong again until she started to talk.

"I'm sorry. I should respect you when you say it makes you feel uncomfortable. It's just that I have feelings for you, and I'm scared that you don't have the same feelings for me."

"Feelings are funny things," I said.

The seventh rule of *The Company Culture Handbook* was to "Always Diffuse Discomfort." The company had taught us that ambiguous or generalized statements were good at this, and though I wasn't sure if it would work on Donna because she'd read the same manual, it did seem to work because she started to nod and smile.

"You know I've liked you for a while, don't you?"

"Yes," I said.

"Then why didn't you ever ask me out?"

I'd wondered the same thing myself sometimes but then I always just preferred to go home and walk Molly and watch television, but I thought she might not like to hear that, so instead I thought again of the seventh rule of *The Company Culture Handbook* and just said, "It's hard to know why anything happens the way it does" and again she nodded and smiled. The fact was that I'd mostly liked to be alone growing up, and there were other incidents between me and other people with me wanting to see them red and open, so I usually didn't spend more time with people than I absolutely had to.

We sat drinking beer and were mostly silent when Donna finally said, "Sometimes I like that you don't talk a lot. It makes it more meaningful when you do speak."

She'd said the same thing on other occasions and I could tell that the alcohol was affecting her because she sometimes repeated herself when she'd been drinking, but it was still nice to hear it because I knew that some people thought I was weird because I didn't talk very much, and I always wanted to tell those people that I just didn't talk much with my mouth but that my mind was always talking, but then I usually didn't tell them this because the few times I did they usually walked away from me with a funny look on their faces.

I also remember once when I was in the fifth grade and a few of us walked to a convenience store at lunchtime, and though I don't remember much about the clerk or the layout or the prices, I do remember that it wasn't much of a convenience store.

Once we got inside, two of the kids bought licorice and the other one bought gum, but I didn't buy candy at all and instead decided to buy a small jar of honey, and even though it was just as sweet and tasty as what they'd bought, it didn't seem to matter because when we left the store the three of them went off on their own and I could hear one of the licorice-eaters saying, "There's always been something a little off about him" to the others. I also remember how I'd brought it up to my parents later that night and how they just told me that in a world where most fifth graders bought licorice or gum or chocolate that if another kid bought honey they might think that's "a little off" because most people are only comfortable when everyone is eating and wearing and talking and acting the same as everyone else, but that I should never change who I was just because most people changed the way they were to fit into a pattern. I don't remember exactly which parent said what or even the precise words they used, but I do remember that was the gist of it.

"I'm glad you like it," is all I said, after I'd finally come out of my remembering.

"Have you always been that way?"

"Mostly," I said. She'd asked me the same thing at least once before, but I didn't mind answering it again.

"Why do you think that is?"

"Why what is?" I said.

"Why are you so quiet?"

"It's hard to say," I said.

This wasn't me trying to invoke the seventh rule of *The Company Culture Handbook* but was in fact the simple truth. I thought about maybe telling Donna about the police officer and how he'd asked me questions about Molly and Sherman Dempsey, but then I thought better about it and instead I asked her if she'd like me to come back to her place, and she said yes and so, after we finished a couple more drinks, we did.

CHAPTER 18

Last night I was unable to achieve it even with Donna's help and she said not to worry about it and that it had happened to most of her boyfriends at one time or another, but none of that was very comforting to me for various reasons.

She said that maybe it was stress related and though I didn't feel particularly stressed I did have some awfully strange dreams during the night and woke up still thinking about the police officer and the landlord and Sherman Dempsey and so maybe Donna was right.

I got home just in time to take Molly for a walk and feed her and get to work. I received a phone call midway through the day, and since Donna put it through to me, I thought it might be a lay-down. Instead it turned out to be the officer that I'd spoken to on two occasions and he asked me if I could come down to the police station and meet with him and his inspector and I told him that I was working and he said that it could wait until after work was finished so then I told him that I had to walk Molly after work was finished and he said that it could even wait until after that so then I finally agreed to meet them.

After I hung up the phone, Donna asked me why the police were calling me, and I told her that they were probably hoping to get help from the tenants in figuring out what happened to the landlord and that since I'd been one of the last to see him I likely had some clues or leads they might be able to follow, and she smiled after I said this but it was a weak smile.

I met with the inspector and the officer at the police station at eight o'clock. They took me into some type of interview room where there was a plain steel table in the center and a few chairs though only myself and the inspector sat down.

"We started to think you weren't coming," said the inspector. He was an older gentleman and he was wearing a hat that I thought was a fedora.

"Why did you think that?" I asked.

"We thought you'd be here right after work," answered the officer, who was standing off to the side of the table and leaning against a wall.

"I said I had to walk my dog first," I said.

"Yes," he said, "but we thought you'd come after that."

"I did," I said.

"Did you walk your dog to the next city?" said the officer.

"No," I said. Then I told them that I had dinner first, but since my kitchen sink is still not working I have to get my water from the bathroom and that takes longer and that I watched the news while eating and only left after the news was over.

"Sir, do you know why we've asked you to be here today?" said the inspector. He took off the hat that I thought was a fedora and rested it on the table.

"You need my help to find the landlord," I said.

"Do you know where he is?" he asked.

"No," I said. I didn't much like lying to police officers, but this was one of those times that I felt it was absolutely necessary.

"You should know that you're not under arrest, and we're not detaining you. You are free to come and go from this room at any time, do you understand that?"

"I understand," I said.

"But you should also know," said the inspector, "that we are investigating a murder and a disappearance and that they both have some connection to you." He pointed his finger rather accusatorily in my direction as he finished the sentence. I felt this was somewhat rude, but then I figured this was probably just his way or maybe even part of his training, so I wasn't too fussed about it.

"Because I found the dead man's dog," I said.

"Yes."

"And because I live where the landlord lived," I said.

"Yes," he repeated.

"Is there a reward?" I asked.

"Come again?"

"I said 'is there a reward?' For finding the dead man's dog?"

I watched as the inspector looked at the officer and the officer shrugged and smiled, and I thought it was weird since I'd asked the question but they were the ones looking at each other and nobody was looking at me, but then soon they were both looking at me.

"There was never a reward for the dog, sir."

"I see," and then I laughed because I'd said "I see" again, and when I did that they both looked at each other again.

"Sir, are you quite all right?" asked the inspector.

"Yes, of course."

"I wonder if you're well. Have you been to see a doctor?"

"Why would I need a doctor?"

After a moment he said, "You understand that we are investigating a murder, don't you?"

"Yes," I said.

"Possibly two," he said.

"Yes," I repeated.

"And you have now confessed to having the murdered man's dog?"

I suppose I had, although I didn't much like him using the word "confessed" since that made it sound like I was guilty of something, and even though I was in fact guilty of something, he couldn't know this for sure, so it seemed rather presumptuous of him to use that word.

"I told this officer that I found the dog and took it home and fed it and then took it to the veterinarian."

"Yes, we've verified that with the neighborhood vet," said the inspector. "He confirmed that part of what you told us."

"That is good police work," I said, and though I meant it sincerely, I suspect maybe they thought I was being smart because both of them smiled in a way as if they hadn't really just received a compliment, which is truly what it was meant to be.

"Thank you for your faith in us," said the inspector.

"You're welcome," I said.

"Sir, I'm going to come right out and say it," said the inspector, "I believe that you know more about both the murder and the disappearance, but you're holding something back. What do you have to say about that?"

Again I tried rule seven of *The Company Culture Handbook* which says "Always Diffuse Discomfort" and said, "What could anyone say to that?" but it didn't work because they just repeated the same question, so then I said, "I don't know what I could possibly tell you that I haven't," and I felt like this wasn't a full lie because even though I did know more, I knew I couldn't possibly tell them more, or else I'd be arrested and lose my job and lose Molly and Donna and would have to go back to achieving it on my own, perhaps forever.

"Do you have any family?" asked the inspector.

"Both of my parents have died," I said.

"Well, I'm sorry to hear that," he said, and he seemed sincere about it. "Anyone else? An aunt or an uncle, perhaps?"

"I had a very small family."

"I see," he said, and even though the inspector had just said "I see" like the officer, I didn't want to laugh because at that moment I was thinking about my parents and about the pets we used to have and how they were all gone now and how it made me rather sad to think of it.

Suddenly the inspector got up from his chair.

"Thank you, sir, that will be all for now."

They walked me out of the police station and watched as I drove away and I drove home thinking that the meeting had gone fairly well and was surprised that I hadn't been more nervous. I then took Molly for a walk and watched some television and then achieved it on my own and then went to sleep.

CHAPTER 19

The next day I was called into Mr. Peters' office and when I walked in, Donna was already sitting there, and he asked me to take a seat beside her and then closed the door.

She had one of her legs draped over the other and it was rocking up and down.

"I spoke to human resources," Mr. Peters said, "and they told me that for the protection of everyone involved, we may need to transfer one of you to another office, in order to diffuse the potential for conflicts."

"I don't understand," I said.

"What it means is that there exists a reasonable apprehension of bias if we have two employees intimately involved in the same location. And neither of you have denied that you're seeing one another."

"What's to deny?" said Donna, and I thought that maybe she was trying to invoke the seventh rule of *The Company Culture Handbook* with an ambiguous phrase, but then she added, "Is it so surprising that employees might date?" and that seemed very much like a confession.

"It isn't," said Peters. "We're all just human. But again, human resources thinks that it would be best for everyone if one of you moved on. I've already been in touch with our next closest office, and they have a spot for a full-time administrative assistant."

"Me?" said Donna.

"Well, they said that—"

"This is such bullshit," she added.

Donna was clearly failing both the first rule of *The Company Culture Handbook,* which was to "Always Stay Positive" and the fifth rule, "Be a Humble Student," which taught us that you could learn from every situation, and you ought to accept change or criticism or coaching with humbleness and understanding and consider it a learning experience.

"You just want to ship me out because you can replace me like this," she snapped her fingers, "but you can't replace a good salesman so easily."

The ninth rule of *The Company Culture Handbook* was "Nobody Likes a Challenger" and I could tell that

Mr. Peters truly believed in that rule because his face became tight and rigid when Donna said this and it was obvious that he didn't appreciate her insinuation, but then it
was just as obvious that Donna felt that the company was
no longer being her friend and was thereby violating the
tenth rule, so maybe it was a wash.

"You know that we value you here, Ms. Wintergrass.
You've been a fine asset to our company for the last two
years, and you will not be as easily replaceable as you
might think."

"And what if I refuse to go?"

He didn't say anything more and then Donna started
to cry, which I found strange because she'd told me she
didn't like this job anyway, but then I figured maybe
she'd just been blowing off steam since it was a difficult
time to be unemployed, and she'd recently been com-
plaining to me about her finances and how she hardly had
enough money to feed Bob the turtle or to fix the strings
on her viola when they snapped.

"I can leave," I said.

I hadn't really thought about it, but then I didn't like
seeing Donna cry, and I didn't much care for most of my
co-workers there anyway and I could sell vacuums all the
same from anywhere even if I had to drive a bit farther to
get to work and then I thought it might even be a good
excuse to move from my apartment building and get
away from the officer and the inspector but then I figured

just as quickly that it might make me look guilty to move so soon after I'd talked to them so I decided maybe I could just commute.

"Well, let's not be so hasty," said Mr. Peters, and I could tell that he hadn't expected me to volunteer to leave, and I saw Donna was smiling now and then Mr. Peters said he'd call human resources once more and investigate if there were any other options and we were both excused from his office and went back to work.

ๆ๛ๆ

By the end of the week the matter had been resolved, and it turned out that neither of us had to leave. Donna was merely moved to a cubicle farther away from my own and was from then on prohibited from processing any of my orders and swore that she would not give any preferential treatment to me and that was how things were settled, "on a temporary basis," as Mr. Peters had put it.

Donna was so impressed with me that she took me out for dinner Friday, and when we went back to my place she helped me to achieve it three times, which was something I hadn't done since I was in college.

CHAPTER 20

On Sunday there was a knock at my door, and when I answered it I found the inspector and the officer there and they asked me if they could come inside and I asked them if they had a warrant which was something that I always heard people ask on television and they said that they didn't but asked if they could come in all the same and then I thought that it was usually just guilty people who brought up the issue of having a warrant and even though I was in fact guilty I didn't want them to think I was—which was funny because I knew they already did—but I invited them in all the same.

Molly was excited to have guests and was whisking her tail in the air and I told them to make themselves at home and to keep their shoes on and they did.

The inspector removed the hat that I thought was a fedora and walked over to my balcony window and slid back the curtain and looked outside. The officer was milling about my main entryway and finally joined the inspector in the main room.

"Just the one bedroom?" asked the inspector.

"Yes."

"May I see it?"

"Of course."

I showed it to him and he looked in the bathroom and then he'd pretty well seen everything except for the closets, so we went back out to the main room, which was connected to the kitchen.

"So this is the dog?" asked the inspector as Molly ran up and rubbed up against his leg as he bent down and scratched her neck.

"That's Molly," I said.

"Jasmine," said the inspector.

"What's that?"

"Her name was Jasmine," said the inspector. "We talked to the deceased's sister and she said that the dog's name was Jasmine."

"Jasmine," I said. I liked that name and thought that maybe Molly would like it if I went back to calling her Jasmine, but then I thought it might be confusing so I decided to just keep calling her Molly.

"Did she say if she wanted her back?" I asked.

"She didn't mention it," said the officer.

Molly was now rubbing up against the officer's leg though, unlike the inspector, he hadn't knelt down to scratch her.

"Why don't you sit?" I said.

We sat in the main room. I sat on the green chair that was going to be Donna's green chair as soon as I replaced it and they sat on the couch. The inspector looked at me but the officer only looked around the room.

"I wonder if you've thought of anything new?" said the inspector. "Anything new since we last talked?"

I told him that I couldn't say anything more.

The inspector smiled and did seem genuinely friendly, which was somewhat surprising, given that he suspected me to be involved in these very serious matters, but the fact that he could remain pleasant seemed very professional of him in my opinion.

"We have been doing some digging," he said. "Just a bit of digging into your past."

"Yes?" I said.

"You are quite right, both your parents have passed on due to cancer. Awful disease. Simply awful."

"Yes," I said.

I wondered how they would have found that information, but then figured it was their job to undercover facts like that and didn't think anything more of it.

"And we checked out some other things. Where you

went to college. Your employment history. Nothing out
of the ordinary, really."

"That's good," I said, but it also felt like the inspector was leading up to something more and by then the
officer had stopped looking around the room and was
looking directly at me and I started to feel nervous for the
first time.

"Nothing as an adult," he said. "Nothing at all as an
adult."

He looked briefly at the officer then back at me.

"But as a *youth*. That is something very different. Six
different schools despite living in the same city?"

"Yes," I said.

"Can you explain that?"

"I was young when I was in school," I said.

"Yes, I'm sure that you were. But do you know why
you would never stay at the same school for more than
one or two years at a time?"

"I couldn't say. I'm sure there are records for that."

"Yes—an interesting thing about youth records,"
said the inspector. "They are sealed up tighter than—
well, let's just say that they are sealed."

"I didn't know that," I said.

"No, no, I wouldn't expect you to. But then I thought
that if I just asked you what might be in those records,
that you, being a very straightforward and cooperative
fellow, as you have been, you might just be willing to tell

us about it. As much as you remember, at least?"

"It was a long time ago," is all I said.

"Mm-hmm," said the inspector.

I knew most of the incidents that were probably in the records. They would have been incidents like when I stuck the stick into the kid's eye or stabbed the girl in the neck with a pencil, but I figured these things would probably just make me seem more guilty to them, even though they were from many years ago and had nothing to do with either man that I'd killed, and I didn't think it would be fair so I decided not to tell them.

"I really don't know," I said. "I guess you could ask the school."

"We did," said the officer. He hadn't spoken for several minutes and had a rather annoyed look on his face.

"If you would just tell us what you remember?" prodded the inspector.

It occurred to me that they were fishing for whatever they could, and I realized they really had no evidence to connect me to any of this, so I figured if I just kept my mouth shut that they probably would never be able to connect me to either one of them and this made me feel much better.

"I really don't remember much from school," I said. "Except that it was boring."

"The landlord," said the inspector. "There's still been no word from him?"

"No," I said.

"What do you think about that?" he said.

"I think that the owner needs to replace him because my sink is still broken."

The inspector looked at me quizzically after I said that and said, "How do you know he's not coming back?"

I felt my neck getting red because I was suddenly very nervous and uncomfortable, and I think maybe Molly was able to sense it because she started to bark and then this just made me more uncomfortable and I could see the inspector still staring at me waiting for my answer and that's when I remembered the seventh rule of *The Company Culture Handbook* which was to "Always Diffuse Discomfort" so I got up and moved to the sink and invited them to come see how no water came on when I lifted the faucet but then I immediately regretted it because I was now showing them the precise scene of the second murder and I started to worry I'd missed a splotch of blood or bone or there might be some evidence I didn't appreciate but then I figured by then it was too late.

The inspector followed me over and I saw him looking strangely at the floor and then I realized that he was noticing how clean the floor was in that area because I'd had to use so much bleach there to scrub out the blood that had come out of the landlord's head.

"Why is the floor like this?"

I opened the cabinet doors beneath the sink and

showed him how it was constantly leaking water there and how I often had to wash that area so maybe that was why it was like that.

He knelt down and ran his finger along the floor.

"Smells like bleach…"

"I suppose it should. I used bleach there."

"Why would you use bleach to clean spilled water?" asked the inspector.

"Sometimes the water is dirty," I said, and it was the truth.

"We could have a team here, you know?"

"A team?" I asked.

"A forensics team," he said.

"I'm sure you could," I said, because I was satisfied that he was not lying to me.

"And do you think we'd find any trace of the landlord here if we did? Any blood or hair?"

I knew he was asking me just to watch my face and see my reaction and it made me a little more nervous, but then I thought of how absurd it all was and I couldn't help but smile, and I could see this wasn't the reaction he was expecting or hoping for because I saw him look over at the officer and now they both seemed annoyed.

"Is something funny?" said the inspector.

"I was just thinking that you probably would find some evidence of the landlord because he's been here to fix my sink before. If your team is good they would probably find something, but if they're not good then I suppose maybe they wouldn't."

"Yes," said the inspector. "I suppose not."

"In fact he's been all through this apartment since I've been here. There might be traces of him all over."

"No doubt," said the inspector, and again he looked at the officer and with a similar look of annoyance.

Then he stuck his head under the sink just as the landlord had when he'd asked me for the flashlight and twice asked me for the wrench. The officer was standing beside me so I knew I couldn't attack the inspector without being attacked myself by the officer, but since I had no feelings to see the inspector red and open, I figured it wasn't an issue.

"How long has it been like this?" he asked.

"For weeks," I said.

"And why didn't you ask for it to be fixed sooner?"

"Before it just leaked. Then the landlord disappeared."

He pulled away from the sink and then stood back up, clapping his hands together to clean them.

"Very unfortunate for you," he said.

"What's that?" I said.

"The timing of his disappearance. Very unfortunate, because now there's nobody to fix your sink."

"Yes, it's unfortunate," I said. "I hope he returns soon."

The officer's face turned red and it seemed as if maybe he wanted to see me red and open, but instead the inspector ushered him to the door where he put the hat back on that I thought was a fedora.

They both stepped from my door before the inspector suddenly turned back to me.

"You know, we never found the tools."

"What's that?" I asked.

"The landlord. Apparently he had a toolbox. We never have been able to find his tools," said the inspector.

"I see."

"Let us hope that the new landlord brings his own tools, if you ever hope to have your sink fixed," said the inspector, then he tipped his hat that I still thought was a fedora and they both left.

CHAPTER 21

I was feeling pretty good the next day because I sold seven vacuums, which was an awful lot, and Donna hadn't put any of them through to my phone line, which meant that I had worked hard for all of them and that there shouldn't be any reasonable apprehension of bias from the other salesmen.

It was also public knowledge by then that Donna and I were seeing one another and that was fine because Jeff and Gary and the rest had finally stopped ogling her, at least in my presence.

But the biggest news from that day was the fact that a man had shown up at the police station to confess to the murder of the missing landlord. It was on the evening news that I was watching after dinner, and it said that a

man had confessed to attacking the landlord for some un-
known slight and then tossing his body into the river.

There was a short news clip that showed the inspector speaking at a press conference behind a podium. It
wasn't much of a press conference, and he was still wearing the hat that I thought was a fedora, only I wasn't so
sure anymore because I'd started paying attention to hats
in shopping windows and in magazines and since there
were so many names and styles of hats, it's possible that I
was mistaken all along. He had a very serious look on his
face and he said that there was still further investigation
required to "verify this man's account of things," which
was to say that the inspector didn't believe him and
thought that the man was crazy, and he was probably
right, given that I knew the man was confessing to a murder that he didn't commit.

The police dragged the river for the next three days
but they didn't come up with the landlord, and it would
have been awfully strange if they had managed to, given
that I'd left bags of him in something of a landfill by the
junkyard.

Donna asked me what I thought about it and I just
told her that "it's hard to know why people do the things
they do," and I said this because it was true, but also because I didn't really want to talk about it and that seemed
to work because she didn't mention it again.

I met the new landlord when I got home and he was

much younger and chubbier than the old landlord, but he was also very friendly to me and shook my hand and his breath didn't smell of alcohol and when I told him that I was happy to see a new landlord because my kitchen faucet didn't work he said he'd fix it while I was at work tomorrow and I immediately liked the new landlord.

∽∾∾

At work the next day I'd sold two vacuums before being called into Mr. Peters' office shortly before lunchtime.

I sat in the seat across from him after he shut the door and then he took a seat behind his desk. From there he just looked at me with a curious look and I figured that he wanted to talk about Donna again, only I didn't mind because I was thinking about how my kitchen sink was getting fixed that day and might even have been fixed already.

"I've got something to confess," he said.

It occurred to me that there'd been a lot of talk and thought about confessions and so it really got my attention when he said it.

"If you want to confess, perhaps you should speak to a policeman?" I said.

Mr. Peters stared at me from behind his desk and his eyes looked even more serious than usual, but then all of a sudden he started laughing like I'd never seen him laugh before, and it was as if I'd said or done something really funny, but since I hadn't done anything but sit down in the chair, I concluded that it must have been from what I'd said, and though it wasn't meant to be a joke, he must have taken it as one, so I waited for him to stop laughing and finally he did.

"Is this about Donna?" I said.

He got the serious look back into his eyes.

"Have you been talking to human resources again?" I asked.

He seemed confused and took a moment to answer and finally shook his head and said, "No—no, not at all," and I believed him.

He leaned forward and put his elbows on his desk, which meant that he was about to say something really serious, so I listened closely, not that I hadn't been listening before.

"You remember when we were last in here? With Donna?"

"Yes."

"Well, I received a phone call not much more than an hour after that. From an inspector at the police department."

"I see."

"He was asking me some questions—questions about you."

He didn't say anything more, so I asked him, "What kind of questions?"

"Oh, just regular stuff. How long you've been working for us. What sort of a person I think you are. That sort of thing."

"The inspector asked this?"

Mr. Peters nodded.

"And what did you tell him?"

"What could I tell them, really? Fact is, I don't know you all that well. You've always been sort of an odd duck, you know? I told him that you're not exactly a walking pom-pom, but that you don't cause any trouble, either, and that's all a boss can ask for. That you're quiet and shy-like. That you mostly keep to yourself. That you're pretty much an introvert."

I didn't say anything else and so he asked, "Aren't you curious?"

"Curious about what?" I said.

"Aren't you curious why a police inspector is calling me and asking questions about you?"

"I suppose that is something to be curious about," I said, and even though it wasn't exactly an answer to his question, he told me anyway after a short pause.

"At first he didn't say why, and I didn't much feel it was my business to ask, but then as it went along I guess I got a little more brave, so I asked him what it was all about, and he finally told me that you were one of the last people to see some man who'd gone missing and that it was their duty to check up on everyone who had recently been in contact with him."

"He was my landlord," I said. "The man who went missing."

"Yeah, well, I didn't know what the hell to make of it all, but I figured I better keep it to myself and now that someone has come forward to confess to this man's murder, I put two-and-two together and *voilà*. So now I don't mind telling you because I guess it doesn't matter anymore. Anyway, sorry I had to keep it from you. But you can understand, it being what it is."

"I understand," I said, but really I was just thinking of how "*voilà*" could be reconfigured to spell "viola" and then I started thinking about Donna again and was wondering when she would help me to achieve it again and Mr. Peters kept talking.

"Maybe you *are* an odd duck, but that doesn't make it right for them to be casting suspicion on you like that. Especially with something as serious as that."

"They're just doing their job," I said.

"Well, I'd like to think that I'd be as understanding as you about it but I can't say that I would be."

"I'm just glad someone has confessed," I said. I said it because it was true.

"Well, I'm glad it's all settled anyway. And to think we were just worrying about an office relationship. Goes to show how quickly the paradigm can shift."

A paradigm shift wasn't actually part of *The Company Culture Handbook* but was general company jargon for how something that looked one way at first could look very different once you looked at it from another angle. Mr. Peters was saying that my office relationship with Donna looked bad to him until an inspector from the local police force called to ask questions about me and a missing person and how quickly he realized that an office relationship was not such a big deal as he'd originally thought when comparing it to cold-blooded murder.

The company was always shifting the paradigm with its employees, too. If it was dreary and rainy outside, they would tell us that it was a great time to call people and sell vacuums because there was nothing to do outside that day and people would just be waiting at home with all the time in the world to speak with you about the latest healthy technology and discuss the advantages of buying a new vacuum system. But then the next day, if it was sunny and beautiful outside, they would tell us that it was equally a great time to call people and sell vacuums because if they answered their phones it showed that they weren't interested in doing anything outside and if they weren't going outside on such a gorgeous day then it must mean they'd be happy to stay inside and speak with you about the latest healthy technology and discuss the advantages of buying a new vacuum system.

They would say the same sort of thing to the people that worked in our retail outlets. Things like, "It's a beautiful sunny day outside, so anyone willing to come inside to shop on a day like this is definitely looking to buy." But then if it was raining they'd say, "Look at how miserable it is out there, anyone willing to come outside on a day like this is definitely looking to buy."

They had the same sort of spiel for when it was snowing or sleeting or whether it was summer, fall, winter, or spring. As far as the company was concerned, whatever day or time or season it was, and whether in person or by phone, was always the best day to sell vacuums. This was actually the second rule of *The Company Culture Handbook*: "Every Day is a Good Day to Buy."

CHAPTER 22

When I got home I found that the new landlord had already fixed my sink, so I could finally make dinner with water from the kitchen, and even if it was the same water that came out of the spouts in the bathroom, it somehow seemed different to me, at least psychologically, so I was pleased that it had finally been fixed.

I knocked on his door to thank him after dinner and when he opened the door I could see that he had cats, and though I didn't entirely trust cats, I was relieved to see that the white chew bone was no longer there.

"I want to thank you for fixing my sink," I said, then realized that he must have indeed brought his own tools since I had disposed of the landlord's tools in the same landfill as his body. Then I thought of how the landlord's body was probably rotting and foul by that point and was maybe even covered with maggots and it made me grateful that I'd only thought of that image after I'd already eaten my dinner. Then I figured that I would have been especially grateful if I'd have eaten rice for dinner that night, only I hadn't had rice for dinner, so although I was still grateful, it was just a regular amount of grateful.

As I was thinking of how grateful I was the landlord said, "Just doin' my job," and it snapped me out of my thinking.

Then I told him, "The last landlord tried to fix it once before, but it didn't work for very long, so I suppose that means he never did fix it at all, but merely tried to fix it and failed."

The new landlord just looked at me when I said that, so I figured I must have said something rather strange, so I thought back on what I'd just said and couldn't find anything all that strange about it, then before I could think on it anymore, the new landlord started speaking again.

"Well, if you find it starts actin' up again, you just come let me know."

"I will," I said then returned to my apartment.

ഇരു

Donna came over that night because she phoned and

said she wanted to see me so I said "fine" even though it was a work night and I normally tried to get to sleep early.

I buzzed her upstairs once she arrived and soon she'd knocked on my door and I let her inside. She shook off her coat and I realized that it must have been raining outside because of how wet it was, and it made me think of the paradigm shift and how she must have really wanted to see me if she was willing to come over when it was raining like that.

We put her coat away and took a seat on the couch and I could tell that something was bothering her, then I thought that maybe it was because I still wouldn't telephone her, and though I thought we were already past that, you could never really tell with women so I figured that I shouldn't discount the possibility entirely.

"I had a visitor today," she said.

"That's nice."

"It wasn't a nice visit," she said.

"I see."

I'd found myself saying "I see" with increasing frequency and while before I found it funny because it seemed as if I was parroting the officer, now I just found it a normal part of my talking.

"It was a police inspector," she said. "He was asking me a lot of questions."

"What sort of questions?"

Donna squinted her eyes together and I could see they were moist, but then she opened them back up and she didn't actually cry and that surprised me because she did cry an awful lot and this certainly seemed like it was going to be another one of those times.

"He was asking me about how long we'd been dating and asking me about certain nights we'd been together and even asked me a little about your movements from a couple years ago."

"I see."

"Why are they asking me these things?"

It seemed to me that there was no point in not telling her, so I told her at least the part about finding Molly on the street two years ago and how it had turned out that Molly's real name was Jasmine and how Jasmine's owner had been killed and how they were now suspicious of me because I happened to have Molly and also lived in the same building where another man went missing. I felt that my explanation was mostly the truth even though I left out the part where I'd actually killed the two people and the fact that their suspicions were actually correct.

"But someone confessed to it?" she said.

"Yes," I said.

"So why are they still asking questions?"

"Who's to say why policemen do the things they do?" I said. This was my attempt to "Always Diffuse Discomfort" but it didn't seem to work.

"I'm scared."

I noticed Donna was staring at my green chair, and it seemed as if her brain was churning rather fiercely, so I got up to get her some beer. I twisted the cap off and handed her the bottle, but she didn't touch it and instead kept her eyes on the green chair.

"I was with you the night he went missing," I said.

"Yes," she said, "I told them that."

"You see? And someone has already confessed to the crime."

"I mentioned that, too, but he didn't seem convinced they had the right person."

"How so?"

"Just some things he said and the way he said them. I think they suspect maybe he's an attention seeker or delusional. They say they're having his fitness assessed through the courts to see if he's crazy."

"I see."

"But then he must be crazy, right?"

I asked her what she meant.

"What I mean is he would be crazy to confess to a murder he didn't commit, right?"

"Yes," I said. "That would be crazy."

"But then if he did actually do it then he'd also be crazy, because only crazy people murder people, right?"

She looked at me expectantly after she'd said it and I wasn't immediately sure how to respond, but eventually I told her that a lot of people kill other people like in the military or policemen or in self-defense or for some other good and justifiable reason.

"What would be a good reason to kill a landlord?" she said.

"Who can say? He drank a lot and he wasn't a very nice man. Maybe he had a lot of enemies."

I had taken a law course in college and one of the things that they taught us was that lawyers would some-times point to "alternative suspects" when they had noth-ing else to go on even though most everyone in the court-room knew that their client was guilty. Pointing to alter-native suspects and other speculative alternatives could muddy the waters and shift the paradigm of the jury at least enough to raise a reasonable doubt, so I thought maybe if it worked on them, it would work on Donna, and it apparently did because she then said "I suppose so."

Another thing they taught us was the defense of "in-nocent explanation." Just as with "alternative suspects," defense lawyers often pointed to innocent explanations when they had nothing else to go on even though most everyone in the courtroom knew that their client was guilty. Our professor gave us the example of a drunk driver, and how the lawyer would suggest that maybe his client's car had swerved off the road because a raccoon had run into the street, and that maybe the ground was uneven and that's why he was stumbling around, and that maybe he was having a stroke or just spoke with a thick accent, so that's why his words sounded slurred and he would go on and on like that and I remember that most of the class had laughed until the professor told us that this stuff actually worked with some sympathetic judges, and then suddenly most of the class stopped laughing. Then one of the students asked how they got to the truth of the matter when counsel put forward such silly arguments, and our professor answered that the law isn't about the truth but is about the process, and so that was the last law course I ever signed up for.

Up to that point I wasn't too sore about the inspector calling my boss or calling the girl I was seeing because I figured that he was just doing his job, and of course I knew that he was right to do so and even righter to be looking at me, so I figured it would be hypocritical for me to get too fussed about it.

Only then I noticed how one of the button's on Donna's blouse had come undone, and I could see part of her bra and the curve of her breasts and it swelled me inside and I no longer wanted to talk about landlords and inspectors so I leaned in and started to kiss her, only she turned away after a moment and put her untouched beer down on the coffee table and said that she better get back home.

She walked quickly to the front closet and grabbed

her coat which was still wet from the rain, and as she put it on I could see that she'd started to cry, so I moved in to kiss her goodnight, but she turned away and I only managed to kiss her cheek and a moment later she was gone.

That was the first night we'd been together that she didn't help me to achieve it.

It was also the first time that I thought of the inspector as red and open.

CHAPTER 23

The next day Donna kept her distance from me. Since this was actually what Mr. Peters wanted I thought that maybe she was just doing it to appease him but then I thought about how our conversation ended last night and figured that would be about as big of a coincidence as Molly's name actually being Molly when I named her that, and since I didn't really believe in coincidences, I concluded that Donna must be avoiding me.

At lunchtime I approached her and asked if she'd like to have lunch with me, which was something I almost never did, but I did it on that day only to be told by Donna that she wasn't hungry. I then discovered that I was no longer hungry myself, and so I didn't eat lunch that day but instead just went back to work. As I was leaving that day I heard my name called aloud, and I turned to find Donna behind me.

I was holding my lunch in my hand and was going to eat my lunch for dinner, which would in a weird way have made it dinner the whole time and not lunch at all.

"Can we talk?"

"Of course," I said. "But we can't talk very long because I have to get home to take Molly out for her walk because otherwise she might—"

"It won't take long," she said, interrupting me.

Her eyes seemed red and swollen, so I figured she must have been crying, or else perhaps she had some allergy I wasn't aware of, but I didn't ask her about it and instead we made our way across the street to a coffee shop.

I ordered a coffee and she just had water and we sat at the back of the room where we could have some privacy. It was small and dark and not much of a coffee shop.

Donna sat across from me and I could see her behavior was tighter than normal because she kept her jacket on and didn't lean her arms over the table to hold my hands, which was something that she liked to do and something that I'd become increasingly receptive to.

"I've been wanting to sit down with you for a few days now," she said.

"That's nice," I said, though the look on her face

suggested that it might not be as nice as I thought.

"You know I've liked you for a long time, right?"

"Yes," I said. I said it because it was true.

"I know it's silly but I'd often thought about how a life with you might be and—" Then Donna stopped talking and sort of waved her hands in front of her as if she was washing away her last sentence or else just didn't know how to finish it. I took a sip of my coffee then and my stomach growled, and Donna must have heard it because she asked if I was hungry, and I said that I didn't feel very hungry, but that maybe my stomach was hungry.

"What is it about you?" she said, smiling.

"What do you mean?"

"You say the oddest, simplest things but they're adorable."

I wasn't sure what made it so adorable because it was usually just the simple truth but I was happy enough that she felt that way about it.

"I have something to tell you," she said.

Given the way that her face and her tone had just turned very serious, I thought that maybe she was going to tell me that she had tested positive for a venereal disease and that I should get myself checked out, and this put a damper on my spirits, but then I immediately figured what was done was done, so there was probably no point in getting too fussed about it.

"I'm glad you wanted to talk," I said. "I thought that maybe you'd been avoiding me."

She reached her hands across the table and took my own in hers, and though I'd been about to take a sip of my coffee I figured I best not disengage at that moment. I then prepared myself for a conversation about herpes or genital warts or maybe even some strange condition I'd never heard of before, but then instead she began talking about the investigation.

"This thing with the landlord has really gotten to me," she said.

"I understand."

"It's just the thought of it, you know? And of course I know you had nothing to do with it, but to even be asked those questions…"

She pulled her hands back and then I felt free to take another sip of my coffee and was rather pleased there'd been no talk of venereal disease.

"I thought about breaking up with you," she said.

"I'm glad that you didn't," I said. I said it because it was the truth.

"But I can't have police officers calling me and asking me these sorts of questions. I just can't—"

She started to cry, and I thought that this might be sort of like when she was holding my hands and that I shouldn't take a sip of coffee, but then I took one anyway.

I felt bad that Donna was feeling this way, and I knew that it was mostly my fault for killing the landlord, but then I also blamed the landlord some because if he hadn't beaten and killed his dog then I never would have had to make him red and open and then there never would have been an investigation into his disappearance and then Donna probably wouldn't be crying now, although she did cry a lot, so it was possible she might have cried today anyway, but just about something different.

"If only I wasn't…"

I took another sip of my coffee as she told me that one of the times she'd helped me to achieve it we'd apparently achieved more than we'd intended because she said she was pregnant, and the moment I heard the "p" word I could feel the liquid get caught up in the back of my throat and it took me an extra second or so before I could swallow. I then thought it might be a good time to diffuse discomfort, but then I figured there was nothing I could say that could really diffuse something like this so I asked her if she was certain.

"I'm sure," she said.

"I see."

"We haven't exactly been careful," she said.

"I suppose we haven't."

I just sat looking at her and then finally she reached out across the table again and took my hands in her own.

"Don't you have anything to say?" she said.

"This will probably make it more difficult to avoid the appearance of conflict at the office," I said.

I thought that she might cry again, but instead she started laughing for the first time that day, and I decided to laugh along with her.

She pulled her hands back again. "I don't know what to do."

"A baby," I said.

"Yes."

"Do you know what it is?" I asked.

"It's far too early to know."

"Of course," I said, even though I didn't know that for sure.

"I would have been so happy, normally—"

Donna looked over at the window, and then so did I, and I could see that it had started to drizzle.

"I don't know what I'm going to do," she said, her head still turned to the window.

"I'm going to be a father," I said. I said it because it was true but also because I wanted to say it.

Donna didn't say anything further. Instead, she abruptly got up from the table and said that she had to leave. I asked her where she was going and she said that she didn't know, then I asked her if I could drive her home, and she said she was "fine," which I knew for a woman meant the reverse, but before I could offer again

she was out the door and twisting her way through the
wind and the rain.

CHAPTER 24

As luck would have it, a man was stabbed to death that night not so many blocks from where I lived. It was not so lucky for the man who was stabbed, of course, but then I thought that it might at least distract the police with a new mystery, but the matter was quickly resolved as a drug-related crime. Then I felt bad about being happy about someone dying just because it might benefit me by distracting the police, but then I remembered it was drug related and figured that, just like my landlord, he probably deserved it.

Donna remained distant at work the next day, and though I had always preferred that she keep some distance, especially after our meetings with Mr. Peters, I didn't want quite as much distance as she was keeping. I tried to block it out and went on selling my vacuums, but I only sold one vacuum that day and then Donna left work without saying goodbye and that was when I decided to go visit the inspector.

ᘒᘓᘒᘓ

I gave my name and then waited on a wooden bench in the police station. After a while I saw the officer come out and whisper something to the receptionist and then he glared at me and went back inside the building.

I waited for nearly forty minutes before the inspector stepped out from a doorway and invited me inside. He led me to his office where he had me sit in a chair in front of his desk, then he took a seat behind it just as Mr. Peters had done when he'd first asked me to stop achieving it with Donna.

"Awfully sorry to have kept you waiting," he said. "Positively unavoidable."

I didn't respond because I was looking around his office. His desk was very plain and there was a bookcase and a filing cabinet and a few little knickknacks here or there, but otherwise it was very ordinary and really wasn't much of an office. He also had a coat rack by the door which held his coat and the hat that I used to think was a fedora until I started looking at hats in shopping windows and magazines. I wanted to ask him to clarify once and for all, but then I figured now was probably not the best time, so I simply concluded in my mind that it was "likely a fedora," at least until I came up with some conclusive evidence to the contrary.

"You might imagine how surprised I was to hear that you'd come to see me. Especially with how we left things last time."

His statement called for more, so I asked him what he meant.

"Well, what with our investigation, of course. Our snooping around your kitchen and some of the questions we put to you. Surely you are aware that we consider you a suspect in your landlord's death?"

"But someone has confessed to the murder," I said.

"Yes, someone indeed has confessed to the murder. And what do you make of that?"

"Why would my opinion matter?"

"Oh, if you would just humor me," he said.

I thought about it and then told him that my opinion was that it was good to have someone like that off the street, so it was a good thing that he came forward.

"So, relief?"

I didn't answer.

"Sir, you felt relief at his confession?"

"I don't think I felt relief," I said. "As I said, it's a good thing to have a man like that off the streets."

"Yes, you may be right about that," said the inspector. "You may very well be right about that in the final analysis."

I heard some shuffling behind the door, and it sounded like some mild commotion, but then the inspector started talking again.

"And to what do I owe the pleasure of this visit?" he asked.

"You have spoken to my boss," I said.

"Yes."

"And you have spoken to Donna."

"Ms. Wintergrass, yes, indeed. Lovely woman."

"It has caused me problems," I said. I said it because it was true.

"Well, I'm awfully sorry about that. Awfully sorry."

He seemed too jovial to be truly sorry, but then I thought maybe that was just his way, so I wasn't too fussed about it.

"It is a murder investigation, after all," he said. "Just doing our due diligence. I'm sure you wouldn't expect any less of us."

"No," I agreed. "Only you have a man who has confessed to the murder."

"Indeed we do," said the inspector.

"Donna is upset," I said.

"That is indeed a shame."

"I want you to leave her alone," I said.

"I bet you do," said the inspector before he wriggled

forward in his chair and looked at me with a rather harsh look.

"She has nothing to do with this," I said.

"Peculiar that you would phrase it that way, sir, that '*she* has nothing to do with this.'"

"She doesn't," I said.

"And what of you, sir?"

"What of me?" I said.

"I mean, can you honestly say that you yourself have nothing to do with this? That you know nothing more than you've told us?"

I told him that I didn't appreciate his implication, and I thought this was a good answer since it was true, and if I'd said that I had nothing to do with it then that would have been a rather bold lie, and I tried to avoid those when possible.

"Do you find it odd, sir?"

"What is that?"

"Do you find it odd that I'm willing to meet alone in my office with a man that you quite well know I suspect of having murdered or been involved in the murder of two people?"

"So you do suspect me?" I asked.

"Isn't it obvious?"

I felt my heartbeat rising in my chest and I thought that maybe I shouldn't have gone there, but then I also figured it was too late, by that point, so there was no sense beating myself up over it. "It is obvious you suspect me of something," I said.

"Well, let me erase any doubt altogether," said the inspector. "I suspect that you killed Mr. Dempsey in the alleyway and then took his dog, and I suspect that you were somehow involved in the disappearance of your landlord."

I didn't respond.

"Aren't you curious, sir, why I would meet alone with a man like that in my office?"

"I'm not," I answered, even though I was.

"Well, I will tell you anyway. I suspect that those two men did not suspect a thing was wrong before it was too late. As far as I can tell, you had only a marginal connection with the landlord and likely no connection at all to Mr. Dempsey. As such I suspect that you managed to get the drop on them, so to speak, before they realized anything was amiss, and before they could do anything about it. But I suspect at the very heart of it you are a coward. A true coward down to your very bones. And I suspect you wouldn't dare try engage someone who was ready for you, and, might I say, readily up to the task."

He wasn't much of an inspector to be saying these things. I hadn't been called a coward since my school days, and I could already feel my ears filling with blood and my heart racing in my chest, and I was going to explain to him that "Nobody Likes a Challenger" but instead I was already starting to imagine the inspector as red and open.

I placed my hand in my pocket as he started to laugh. I could tell he was trying to goad me into doing or saying something, and I knew that I ought not do either, but I was already thinking of how good it would feel to punch him in the face and to see him knocked back behind his desk and how I'd like to sink my knife into his throat and stab him over and over and over again until his neck had been completely split open and was gushing blood and I could see the back of his throat and neck.

Hand in my pocket.

"Sir?"

Red and open.

I'd started into my breathing exercises by then and I could barely even hear him speaking. I closed my eyes, and he called my name again but I ignored it. I tried to imagine the consequences of my actions, which is what my parents and teachers used to tell me, so I imagined how the other police officers would surely storm into the office when they heard the commotion and beat me into submission but by then it would be too late and I would be charged with the murder of the inspector and there would be no getting out of that one and how I'd likely be killed by lethal injection or sent to the gas chamber and then my son or daughter or both if Donna had twins would have to grow up without a father, and even if I wasn't much of a father how it would still be better than not having one at all.

I thought of all these things and knew I shouldn't react but the feeling to see the inspector red and open was too powerful so I squeezed the object tighter in my pocket then rose to my feet and opened my eyes and only then noticed the picture on his desk and it jarred me just long enough to interrupt my cycle of scary thoughts and, before I knew what had happened, I said to the inspector, "I'm going to be a father."

This seemed to take him by surprise, because he leaned back in his chair and smiled. "Congratulations," he said.

"Donna told me yesterday," I added.

I kept my hand in my pocket and continued to stare at the picture and do my breathing exercises and think about Donna being pregnant with a son or daughter or both if she had twins.

The inspector said nothing more. Finally, I said, "I have nothing more to say to you."

I'd only taken two steps toward the door before he called out to me. "Sir, aren't you at all interested in why I haven't arrested you for these offences?"

I told him that I wasn't, which was my second bald-faced lie to him in so many minutes.

"Evidence," he said. "Just not enough evidence." He paused before adding, "*At this moment.*"

"A man has confessed," I said.

The inspector smiled and nodded. "Indeed a man has confessed," he said. "A street person. A man who howls at the moon."

"A street person can murder," I said.

"Yes, they can."

"A man who howls at the moon can murder."

"Yes. Certainly, he might murder the moon, at least," said the inspector.

"You should be careful with him," I said.

"Oh, I don't think that will be a problem," he said. "I don't think that will be a problem at all. You see, the man is quite stone dead."

I didn't know how to respond to this so I decided not to.

"Tragic thing really. Hung himself just before you arrived here. Bedsheets. Only so much we can do, really. Shoelaces, razors. Eventually if a person wishes to do themselves harm, it seems they find a way."

"Perhaps he was feeling guilty," I said.

The inspector just stared at me. Finally, he said, "If you would like to know why I haven't charged you, sir, on the one hand, I have you finding a dead man's dog on the street, which is rather suspicious but not a crime, in and of itself, and of course you not knowing that man you would have no motive whatsoever to do him harm, so there is the one."

"There is the one," I said.

"And for the landlord, we have a man fully confessed who has now hung himself dead in our cells and can never recant his claim of responsibility. And so there is the second."

"Yes," I said.

"Now what are the chances, without more, that a jury might convict a man faced with each of those scenarios?"

"I couldn't say."

"I will tell you myself," said the inspector, finally rising out of his own seat and stepping out in front of his desk. "They would say that we were crazy. They would question the mental health of our department. It would become a circus. We cannot convict someone on mere suspicion, sir, no matter how suspicious that person may be."

"I see."

"Now," he added, "if the real killer were to admit what he'd done—if he were to come forward and accept some level of responsibility for these crimes, then perhaps that would be different—"

"Perhaps," I said.

"And what do you think about that, sir? What do you think are the chances that the person truly responsible for these crimes might come forward and confess their sins?"

I decided to assault him with honesty. "I would say that the chances are not good."

The inspector crossed his arms and leaned back against his desk as I stood there by the door with one hand still in my pocket. "No, I suppose not," he said, and then he watched me as I left.

It was only after I'd stepped out of the building that I finally pulled my hand from my pocket, and it was rather sore in one spot, and I turned my hand over and looked at the bottom of it and saw the deep impression of a Polar Bear set snow white into the meatiest part of my hand, and I saw how red the blood was around the impression and how it was just as red as I'd imagined the inspector's throat before I'd noticed the picture on his desk.

CHAPTER 25

In the days that followed, things slowly returned to normal and Donna said she wanted to keep the baby and wanted to be with me, and so we found a house together and even though it wasn't much of a house, it meant that both of us got to keep the green chair, so I think at least that part worked out for the best.

Eventually my son was born and by then Donna had been transferred to a different location within the company, but she was okay with it because a member from human resources had met with her personally and explained how it was best for everyone involved and Donna seemed to accept this without much difficulty.

I continued to sell vacuums with newer healthy technology, and even if the technology didn't really change all that much from year to year, it seems that I was still able to sell enough vacuums to pay for a family and a dog and a turtle named Bob who would die before long, but I still paid for him while he was alive.

I also continued to follow the local newspapers, and I never read anything about Mr. Dempsey or the landlord again, which meant that the landlord's body was surely never found and was likely still rotting in the landfill unless animals had gotten to it, but either way it seemed to me very likely that the matter had been put to rest because the inspector left me alone after that. I did, however, see the officer once, so I waved "hello" to him from across the street but he must not have seen me because he didn't wave back.

After the man hung himself in the cells, Donna seemed satisfied that he must have done so from a guilty conscience, and since the inspector stopped calling her and asking her questions, she must have satisfied herself wrongly of my innocence, and though I didn't like to see her ignorant like that, I felt it was better than the alternative. Still, for a time I strongly considered retrieving what was left of the landlord and depositing him in the river, in the hopes that he might wash up and corroborate the dead man's confession, but then I figured that if I was intercepted before I got to the river and was discovered carrying bags filled with decomposed parts of my former landlord, then it might be hard to come up with an innocent explanation and how even the most sympathetic judge probably wouldn't let me off the hook on that one, so I decided not to risk it.

Our son's name was Toby and I thought that was a good name because I'd never met a Toby that I didn't like and neither had Donna so we both felt rather confident that we would like our son and, as time went on, we certainly did. He was a bright and happy boy and talked often and was rarely sullen and though some of his outside parts looked like mine he was nothing like me on the inside and though this might have been a source of disappointment for some parents, it was, in fact, a great relief to me that he had taken after Donna much more than he'd taken after me.

So in those early years it was just me and Donna and Toby and Molly and Bob the turtle until he died, and even if it wasn't much of a house, I think what was inside the house was all pretty good.

My life had somehow settled me in a way that I'd never been settled before. I would rarely think of anyone as red and open again, and even when I did, I would immediately start into my breathing exercises and consider the consequences of my actions. Most of the time this worked. Sometimes it didn't, but I don't much like thinking about that. I prefer thinking of my family and Molly and the other pets we would have during our life together, which even included a cat, and though I never entirely trusted the cat, we got along well enough, all things considered.

Donna would often say how we'd be together forever and I didn't know about that because forever seemed like an awfully long time but then she said it with such conviction that I figured maybe she knew what she was talking about.

She would also tell me often that she loved me and would then ask me if I loved her in return and this seemed an odd torture since I never seemed to answer satisfactorily because she would sometimes cry as she often did but then she wouldn't cry for long and would keep saying those same three words to me so I guess my answers weren't so bad, all things considered.

That Donna loved me was clear, and it was something I hadn't felt from a person since my own parents and though we would sometimes have fights or arguments, it was usually as a result of my not sharing what I was thinking or not showing any emotion, but then rather than try to "Control the Conversation" I would "Assault her with Honesty" and just explain to her that I was thinking and sharing a lot of emotion in my head but that it was difficult for me to express it in words, and then she would usually hug me and apologize, and if Toby was asleep or in bed, she would help me to achieve it and it would soon be forgotten, at least until it happened again.

With all the people and the animals around it was

much harder for me to be alone with my thoughts, but when I did get the chance I would often think back on how close I'd come to myself being red and open, only in a different way, by lethal injection or gas chamber. But it seems that the inspector had been telling the truth in that they did not have further evidence against me on either case, and since the landlord's body was never found perhaps they finally accepted that the confessor was the real killer and that the landlord's body had indeed been washed somewhere down the river, but either way, neither the inspector or the officer bothered me again, and that was good enough for me.

I would also sometimes think back to the two men I'd killed, and though I did feel some remorse for what I'd done, I also felt that they'd mostly deserved it and that it wouldn't have been right for me to confess and end my own life in the process, so I usually didn't feel too remorseful for too long.

But perhaps most of all I would think back to how close I'd come to making the inspector red and open when I was at the police station and clenching the Swiss Army knife with the Polar Bear handle in my pocket that I'd already opened to the large blade even before I'd arrived because I didn't want to risk opening it up to the file by mistake such as when I killed Mr. Dempsey, and though I felt it may have been silly to bring one of the murder weapons into the police station, it was small and fit easily in my pocket and so it was very convenient.

That I'd managed to control myself was fortunate because I figured my life would have turned out very differently had I done what I was about to do when I stepped up from the chair and I figure I would have likely gone ahead with it had I not seen the picture on the inspector's desk of him and his son in some sort of park and how they were both smiling and happy, and it momentarily gave me pause, given that I might be having a son of my own, or a daughter, or one of each if Donna had had twins, which she didn't.

Only then had I looked a bit lower in the picture and seen their Golden Retriever and he looked so happy and healthy as his tongue wagged out of his mouth and with his coat thick and shiny, and I remember how I instantly knew that the inspector didn't deserve it, even if he had been trying to goad me into confessing to a crime he couldn't prove and had caused Donna some mild distress.

He might not have been much of an inspector, but he certainly didn't deserve it.

END

ACKNOWLEDGMENTS

I want to thank my beta-readers who more or less all agreed that I came up with something rather unique and these include Brittany Medeiros and Michelle Roth and Eva Braja and my colleague Emily Beaton and my brother Eric and my parents Bob and Mary and also my other colleague Adam Bernstein, who even read it while on an airplane on his way to vacation, and even though they likely all had better things to do with their time than to read my story, I suspect they likely received at least some small satisfaction out of it and might even appreciate seeing their names here in the acknowledgment section, and even though it's not much of an acknowledgment section, I think maybe they'll appreciate seeing their names in here, all the same.

About the Author

Michael Paul Michaud is an author and lawyer in the Greater Toronto Area. An American-Canadian citizen, he holds a B.A. in English, Honors B.A. in Political Science (summa cum laude), and a J.D. in Law. He has also made regular appearances on SiriusXM Radio's "Canada Talks."

The Introvert is Michaud's second release. His debut novel, Billy Tabbs (& The Glorious Darrow) was published in November 2014 by Bitingduck Press.

An unabashed zealot of *Animal Farm*, Michaud's chief literary influence is the legendary George Orwell.

fb.com/michaelpaulmichaud

Printed in Poland
by Amazon Fulfillment
Poland Sp. z o.o., Wrocław